ENGAGED TO THE MOUNTAIN MAN

COURAGE COUNTY CURVES

MIA BRODY

1

AURORA

"I KNEW I'D FIND YOU HERE." VIOLET CLUCKS HER tongue against her teeth.

I blink up from the ribbons and sewing supplies carefully arranged on the table across from my canvas. It seems like I've been painting for a few minutes but given the way Violet's lips are drawing down, perhaps not. Perhaps it's been much, much longer. I often lose track of time when I'm here.

"You're meant to meet with the king at four o'clock," she reminds me. She always calls Father the king, as if I might somehow forget his royal status. Or mine.

I set my paintbrush down and give the canvas one last look. It could be hours or days before I make it back into my secret hideaway in the dusty tower to work on my art. It's the bane of every artist's existence—that real life intrudes and keeps us from doing the one thing that makes our souls sing.

She takes me by the arm, the only one who touches me. Even Father's bodyguards aren't allowed to touch me.

I follow her down the old stone corridor. I shiver with a chill, but it has nothing to do with the cold stones beneath my feet. Sometimes, when I'm in certain parts of the castle, I feel them. The spirits of my ancestors, the ones who made noble sacrifices to ensure that my kingdom would continue to be free. For over one hundred and fifty years now, Velkan has known peace.

"Where are your shoes?" Violet chides as we move from the dimly lit corridor into the plush carpeting of the royals' entrance. I suspect royals shouldn't be allowed to get their feet cold.

"I lost them in the garden at the tea party." I look down at my toes. They're leaving dirt streaks on the thick, white carpet. But there is no time to stop and apologize to the maids that will turn the messy floor spotless again.

"How can you forget to wear shoes?" She sounds thoroughly exasperated with me, reminding me of my mom. She died when I was thirteen. Both Violet and I miss her terribly. Violet used to be her assistant and when she passed, I inherited her. The sixty-nine-year-old assistant is like a grandmother to me. She watches over me and arranges my days, making sure my hair and makeup are always appropriate for every occasion.

I don't bother to explain to Violet that none of the other girls were wearing shoes. We took them off to walk barefoot and chase butterflies through the garden. The monthly tea party for underprivileged girls is the highlight of my carefully organized social calendar. It's a chance to learn more about the people that the kingdom exists to serve, and I hold those moments close.

"Is Father in a good mood?" I whisper to her as she knocks on the door.

The slight twitch in her left eye is the only tell. It means he's irritated today but no more than usual. Running a kingdom is serious business. He likes to remind me of that frequently.

When she's granted permission, Violet reaches for the doorknob. I can't remember the last time I touched a doorknob. Maybe not ever in my whole life. There are things that princesses don't do. Things that others do for them.

Sometimes, late at night, I have these wild and

crazy thoughts. Thoughts of running away and becoming a simple man's wife. I'd live on his farm, and we'd work the land together. We'd have a dozen children and three dogs. We'd grow old, hands held as we sit on the porch swing every evening, and I would know freedom from this cage I'm in.

The moment the doors open, Father stands from his desk and gives me a once over. I pretend not to notice the way his lip pulls down in a disappointed frown. Seems I'm a perpetual disappointment to the man, the same way my mother was. They had a cold marriage, one that was on the best days emotionally distant. On the worst, it was cruel, filled with cutting remarks. I shiver to think that might be my future one day.

I hurry into the room. Father doesn't like to be kept waiting. My purple dress swishes with every movement. It's dotted with small paint spatters. After the tea party, I was itching to paint but I knew if I paused to change, Violet would quickly whisk me away to the next event on the day's schedule.

I bow and offer him a warm smile. Twenty-one years and you'd think I'd have the common sense to stop trying for his affection. But some part of me is always hopeful that one day I'll smile at him, and he'll smile back.

He offers me no smile and rounds the large mahogany desk to move to the sitting area where a cart of tea is already set out. He looks pale again today, I note as he takes a chair. I've tried to figure out what's going on but whenever I press Violet for news, she says nothing. Sometimes, all the things I'm not told gather in the pit of my stomach and form a ball of nerves so tight that it's hard to eat or think or breathe.

I pour him hot tea and settle him with the dainty cakes he likes, careful not to spill anything on his suit. The slightest mistake must not be tolerated. We can't look anything less than perfect, not according to Father.

I take a seat too and don't nibble at the dainty treats on my plate. It makes Father happy when he thinks I'm trying to lose weight. I like my curves just fine. My body lets me chase butterflies through the garden and paint beautiful masterpieces. It cushions my bones when I fall, and it jiggles when I full belly laugh.

"Must you always look so unkempt?" He starts the moment I'm seated. "You'll never be desired by your future husband if you don't care for yourself."

My heart pounds as a wave of nausea sweeps through me. Father wants me to be married, and he's been bringing it up this past year. It adds to my worries that something is seriously wrong with his health.

I'm betrothed to a man named Rafael. I've never laid eyes on him, and the union was decided when we were babies. "I've been talking to him."

Technically, that's true. I have left him several voice messages over the past six weeks. He never gets back to me, so I've taken to leaving him long, rambling messages about my hopes, dreams, and fears. I'm treating the calls like a voice diary.

"You still haven't convinced him to join you at the palace." Father is using the stern tone I recognize from his many negotiations.

There is nothing that King Frederic the Fourth has not been able to accomplish while he's on the throne. If he told the sun to stop shining, it would listen. He has that kind of presence and power.

I don't think Violet has given me the right number at all. But I won't point that out and risk getting her in trouble. As it is, I have serious questions about how my prince ended up living in America for so long after seeming to disappear from existence. It's another thing that Violet hasn't explained to me. "I'm trying to get to know him before the ceremony."

Father frowns. He didn't even meet my mother until the day they were wed. He made her miserable throughout their marriage. She spent almost two decades trying to win his heart and never succeeded.

He opens his mouth to continue his lecture but one of his attendants appears from the shadows. He bows before announcing Father has a call of great importance, adding it's the one he was expecting.

Father stands and straightens his suit, scowling down at me the entire time. "Don't overindulge on the pastries."

I recognize a dismissal when I hear one, and I'm relieved that our monthly tea was cut short. I get to my feet and bow one final time before leaving the room without a backward glance.

"YOU HAVE TO GO TO HIM," VIOLET SAYS THAT NIGHT in my bedroom. All of my maids and attendants have been dismissed for the day.

"Go to who?" I fight a yawn as I comb my wet hair. I get my dark hair and eyes from my mother. I've seen pictures of her when she was my age. We could have been twins.

"Rafael. Bring him to the palace. He must take his

place, so that you can take yours." She pauses to set her tablet on my vanity table and pulls off the black frames she always wears. When she does, I realize how dark those circles are under her eyes.

"I don't think I can kidnap him, even if he is my betrothed," I joke to lighten the mood.

"Your father is ill," she confesses.

Suddenly, her insistence on going to Rafael makes sense. There's a law in Velkan. A stupid, archaic one that demands I wed before assuming the throne. If not, it passes to the next heir. My cousin, Nico.

Thinking about the man causes another wave of nausea. He's a notorious womanizer despite being married to a sweet girl. He gambles exorbitant amounts of money, and he's always at the latest nightclubs.

He's not likely to grow up, even if he's handed the kingdom. No, my cousin will destroy the country within a few years. He'll create soaring national debt and make enemies of our closest allies.

But he's been trying to win the hearts of our citizens and get their public support. He thinks that I don't see what he's doing. He's trying to become the next leader, to show that he's the king that cares for them. Except he doesn't.

The moment he's on the throne, he won't concern himself with lowly matters like rising poverty among our elderly or underprivileged girls in dire need of better educational opportunities. All he'll care about is chasing around the maid with the shortest skirt.

"Are you sure?" I ask, my mind spinning. My father's illness means my single days are numbered. I can't sacrifice the security and wellbeing of the citizens, even if a marriage comes at the cost of my own personal happiness. Still, I'd hoped for more time.

She flattens her lips, the way she does when she's debating what to say. Finally, she offers, "Nico doesn't just have the hearts of the people. He has your father's ear."

"And father wishes for him to be next in line," I fill in the blanks. Of course, he does. My father has never made a secret of his disdain for me and my mother. Never hidden how much he's hated the both of us.

"I'll do whatever it takes to get Rafael here." My words may be confident but the knot in my stomach grows. I've promised I will live in this gilded cage forever.

"It's important no one knows about this," she whispers. "If word gets back to Nico…"

He'll use it against me. Look at the princess, shirking her duties while her father is ill. How can such a young, foolish girl be trusted to run the country?

My mind spins with a thousand different ways to explain my absence. Still, I stand and gather myself. "If questioned, you'll say I've been at the girls' home."

Her chin trembles. Only twice I have seen this woman cry. Both times it was for my mother. "You have to travel alone, as a regular citizen. You will announce Rafael publicly before the king and Nico can thwart the marriage."

I give her shoulders a squeeze. She's spent her life reassuring me and today, we're switching roles. I am no longer the child she needs to calm. Now I am the future queen, and it is my job to soothe her. "I'll return within a week with my groom."

2
RAFE

"WHAT'S WRONG WITH YOU?" A SULLEN VOICE ASKS over my shoulder.

My skin is too tight. It's too itchy, and I'm trapped on this metal tube that I can't escape for another two hours. I try to remind myself that this will be over soon, but that does nothing to ease the tightness in my chest.

I don't look at the young girl who's spent the last hour kicking the back of my cramped plane seat. Still, when I speak, I manage to keep the irritation from my voice. She's a kid. "Nothing's wrong with me."

"Your hand is freaky," she announces in a loud tone.

The other passengers pretend not to be listening,

but I see the subtle glances my way. They were there when I boarded the plane too. When you're different, people look at you with a mixture of pity—glad that they aren't afflicted with the same problem and curiosity—insatiable for exactly why you're different.

The cabin is getting smaller. Smaller and hotter. It was this way as a kid too. When the orange glow would get to be too much, my lungs wouldn't hold any air.

"I'm different," I wheeze. I don't usually explain that cerebral palsy makes my arm twist in dystonic postures. But the questions from kids are the ones I try to answer. They need to be shown that people with disabilities are just people. People like them.

Still, I glance back at the kid's mom and silently will her to shush her daughter. To stop putting me on display in front of all these people, like I'm a lion at the zoo. They're tapping at the glass, demanding I perform.

The woman doesn't even meet my gaze. Instead, she idly swipes her tablet screen, ignoring her daughter's behavior the way she has for most of the morning.

"Why are you different? Is it cont—conta—catching?" She settles on the word after failing to pronounce contagious. "Mommy says some things aren't catching. Like when she bleeds from her lady parts. Do you bleed?"

The discussion snags her mom's attention, and she quiets her daughter as some of the other passengers snicker. Just like that, I'm relieved to no longer be the center of attention.

Three hours later, the fingers of my good hand drum an impatient rhythm against the steering wheel. I relax when I cross over into Courage County. I roll down the window, breathing in the pine scent. This tiny town is my new beginning. I've found friends here. I even spent the last few days in Vegas, celebrating a friend's wedding.

I'm glad for Blade. I'm glad he's claimed his forever with Gwen. He deserves every bit of happiness, but something about seeing them together only amplified this feeling. It's a hollow ache deep in my chest. It got even louder on the plane back home. Louder again when I was at the airport, surrounded by the crowd.

My truck dashboard lights up with a call from an unknown number, interrupting my thoughts. Except it's not an unknown number. I know exactly who's calling me.

It's her, a scammer who claims to be a princess in

a foreign country I've never heard of. I don't answer the calls, but I do listen to the messages she leaves.

She says she needs to speak to me urgently. I'm sure it's a con game. She probably means to make me think I've won some money if I'll pay her a small processing fee of a few hundred dollars.

But I can't deny that I've saved each voice message and replay them endlessly on loop. It's the stuff dreams are made of. Breathy and innocent. Every time I hear it, I imagine what she would sound like beneath me.

Against my better judgment, I press accept on the call. Maybe I'm tired of this game of cat and mouse. Maybe I want to hear her voice in real time. I want to know if it's actually as arousing as I think it is.

"Hello," I growl out the word and wait. I'm rewarded with the sound of a voice that's far more musical than her messages.

"I reached you," she exclaims.

"So, you did," I grunt and squirm in the seat of my truck, trying desperately to ignore the semi that I'm starting to sport. She shouldn't be able to do this to me with the sound of her voice, but it feels like a physical caress.

"I'm calling about an urgent matter." Her voice is so prim, reminding me of a schoolteacher or sexy librarian. Shit, that thought goes straight to my cock, and I lose the battle with the semi. Now, it's a raging hard-on.

"Feel free to share *all* your urges with me." I can't resist teasing her. Some part of me feels like I was made to tease her, to annoy her, to arouse her.

She ignores my innuendo or misses it entirely. "Will you be available to me this evening?"

I think of the ways I could make myself available to her and grunt because if I open my mouth and say what's in my head, well, she'll never call again. But maybe that wouldn't be such a terrible thing.

"I request your presence at the airport," she continues.

"I demand your presence in my bedroom," I say before I can stop myself. Apparently, I have no filter. Ah, what the hell. Not like she'll ever call me again after this.

She snorts and calls me a dirty name under her breath. It shouldn't turn me on more, but it does. I imagine her eyes shooting daggers as she calls me filthy things. I'd take her lips under mine. I'd teach her a thing or two about what happens when she calls me names.

"What is this matter regarding?" I ask as I imagine her in my room. Bent over. Tied to my bed.

Screaming for release as I drill deep. All of the filthy images flash through my mind.

"I'm afraid I can't speak of the matter over the phone. It's important that we meet in person."

"Naturally," I growl the word. She's not going to show up. She's making a fool of me. But I'll play along if it means I can hear her voice for a few more minutes.

"Where would you like to meet?" I ask, thinking of all the urban legends I've heard. Isn't this one of them?

Clueless moron gets seduced by a beautiful woman only for his bank account to be wiped clean and all of his assets taken.

"You may escort me from the airport," she answers.

"Shall I bring the limo or the Rolls-Royce?" I do my best to sound bored and unaffected by the conversation.

"Your usual mode of travel will be acceptable to me."

She sounds so formal. I can't help wanting to shake her up. "What shall I tell my driver you'll be wearing? Something sexy, I presume."

"Something travel appropriate," she answers, a definite coldness creeping into her tone.

"Pity," I murmur, wondering what the scammer looks like. Dating isn't really my thing, probably because people aren't my thing. But maybe with a sweet little thing...no, what am I doing? Asking to become her next victim, that's what.

Shaking my head at my silly thoughts, I say, "Be sure to text me your flight information. I look forward to our meeting, princess."

I end the call without waiting for her response. I can't wait to see how she escalates the game next. *She'll probably call and tell me her flight was delayed.*

"AND FOR THE SOPHISTICATED PALATE, SLUGS, crickets, and some leafy greens," I announce to Herbert as I add the food to his enclosure in my backyard. The box turtle had been injured on the side of the road when I found him two years ago. While I don't believe in moving wildlife from its natural habitat, Herbert wouldn't have survived much longer if he'd been left on his own.

"She didn't come, Herb. But we knew she wouldn't. Yep, just two bachelors here. Two *happy* bachelors." I stress the word happy in case he has any doubts about that part.

He doesn't bother to move from the shallow form he dug for himself. He'll stay there overnight. In the daylight, he'll begin to search out the dinner I've added to his enclosure. I did my best to mimic the forest surroundings he must have come from, but still, sometimes I wonder if he ever misses home. Does he remember his?

I try to think back to my first one. Did I have parents who loved me, who wanted me? Nothing exists about my past before age five, so I don't know who I come from. I've been alone for most of my life, other than Herbert.

As I predicted, the princess texted earlier tonight to let me know her flight was running late and we'd have to meet later. I bet anything, I'll wake up tomorrow morning with a text that says her flight was canceled. She'll probably say she needs money or something to get into the States. Yeah, that sounds like the kind of con she's going to play. Good thing I'm no fool.

Still, I can't help wondering why she's targeting me. Does she know about my winnings? I've lived a simple life since then and no one knows about my money except Roman, a friend who lives on this mountain too.

"We're overthinking it again," I tell Herbert as he

continues to ignore me. This is why I love him. He hates people and socializing as much as I do. Yeah, he's the perfect pet for a grumpy mountain man. "Enjoy your food, buddy."

I re-attach the net over his enclosure. It'll protect him from birds that might prey on him. Then I move inside to my cabin, leaving behind the rainy, dreary sky. I wish I could shake off my melancholy mood as I putter around for the rest of the evening before I head to bed. The sheets are itchy against my skin, and the room is too hot.

Something's wrong. It takes me a minute to figure out what this is. I'm craving her. I'm curious about the princess and where she comes from. I want to know what leads a woman to get in her line of work, trying to seduce strange men for their money.

I try to recall the country she claimed to be from. Was it Venice? Valencia? No, that wasn't it. As I'm pondering how many countries can possibly start with a V, there's a loud racket on my porch.

Someone is knocking at my door. I glance at my phone before I push out of bed. There are no text messages or missed calls. None of my friends from the mountain should be here. If they did need help, they would have tried to contact me by phone first.

For a moment, I wonder if it's Mrs. May. May Weatherford is a local woman who has lived on these mountains her whole life, but lately, she keeps getting lost on the way home. Twice this week, in fact. I suspect she's lonely and looking for an excuse to drop in on her neighbors.

I shove into a pair of blue jeans and don't bother to button them. Moving to the door, I call out, "Lost your way again, did you?"

But when I swing open the door, it's not the face of a weathered old woman I'm staring into It's a strange woman. She's beautiful with curves for days, her wet clothes plastered to her body and outlining her shapely figure.

Rain droplets cling to her eyelashes. Her teeth are chattering, and she looks madder than a wet hen as she seethes, "You never met me at the airport."

I blink, certain I misheard her. Then what she said finally makes sense in my brain. Holy shit, this is the fake princess. *She's really here to see me.*

3
AURORA

I can't stop my teeth from chattering as I slog up the mountain. My heels were abandoned over a kilometer ago and now mud squishes between my toes with every step. I am going to murder Rafael for this. He promised me he'd be there.

"What kind of man am I marrying?" I ask the heavens. A streak of lightning flashes as thunder booms. Is this weather an omen? Is it warning me away from a man that can't even keep his word?

A gust of wind sends another shiver through my body. I wouldn't be here if I weren't desperate. Sure, I could pluck any man from the kingdom and marry him, decreeing him the king who will rule beside me. But I know Nico. He'll challenge the validity of the marriage if I don't show up on the arm of my betrothed.

I think of all the girls from the tea party yesterday. They're counting on me. Thousands of families depend on the charity programs that I've implemented in the kingdom. Sure, most of the media likes to act as if I'm a ditzy princess only interested in her latest paintings, but I don't care about what they think. It doesn't matter if the world hates me as long as I can be there for the citizens that need me.

What will Rafael be like as a leader? What kind of king will he be? Though it's my kingdom that he's marrying into, by royal decree we will rule it together.

I think again of his voice and the way it was raspy over the phone. Hearing it made my stomach flutter. Could it be possible that we could one day grow to love each other? Would we have a warm and happy marriage?

As I think the thought, my suitcase hits a pothole, and the latch gives way, sending my clothing all over the muddy road.

I make a pitiful noise of defeat. I could spend the next hour trying desperately to gather all of my clothes that the wind is flinging in every direction.

Or I could make it to that cabin in the distance. The one with the lone porch light on.

I thought I was close to Rafael's cabin when I began at the base of the mountain, but this thunderstorm has my sense of direction going haywire.

My teeth are chattering, so I opt for the cabin. I can always send Rafael out to gather my things later. Maybe it would be good penance for the man given the way he abandoned me at the airport.

Part of me hopes something important kept him from seeing me while another part hopes that nothing bad has happened to him.

Thunder cracks again as I pat the carry-on bag over my shoulder. At least, I had the good sense to keep a small bag on my person with a cellphone that works in the States and a few essentials like my passport.

I pick up my pace scurrying to the porch. I bang on the door as hard as I can with my fist when I don't see a bell. All I want at this point is a hot meal and dry clothes.

I've been traveling all day, across many time zones. I'm exhausted and if I'm being honest, a little hurt that Rafael didn't care enough to show up.

As if I summoned him, the door swings open and there stands a big mountain man. I recognize those piercing blue eyes from the photo I've seen of him. My blood boils and I point a shaking finger at him as I manage to grit out, "You never met me at the airport."

Rafael gasps like I've struck him. "You're the woman from the con."

"No, it's Velkan. Like a soda can." I stress the name of my country slowly. OK, I'm not normally a jerk to people. But standing here in the pouring rain, shouting to be heard over the tempest outside, well, I can be forgiven for being a little bit angry.

"If you were going to make up the name of a country, it shouldn't sound so damn close to Vulcan," he spits out, as if he has any right at all to be upset. What is it with this man? First, he's rude on the phone. Now, he's rude in person.

I push past him and march into the cabin. Manners dictate that I should wait for an invitation, but this man is my fiancé, so really, I'm saving him the trouble of inviting me in. I turn to him and scowl, feeling my cold, wet dress cling to my back.

He doesn't offer me a towel. Doesn't even seem upset that I'm standing here dripping on his hard-wood floors and tracking in mud. "If you were going to con me, you should pick a country name that at least sounds believable."

"What is it with you Americans and your rudeness?" I brush the fringe from my eyes. Why do I have to think that his eyes are as clear as the lake behind Father's castle? Why do I have to notice the way he smells like cedarwood and spice and *home*?

"If there's a country you don't know the name of, then it mustn't exist. So typical." I scowl back at him, suddenly aware that he's shirtless. He's shirtless and so very built. His body looks like it was carved from stone. Except that one arm is twisted up, at a strange angle. One that can't be natural and for a second, I soften. Maybe he has a reason for being a little bit grumpy.

He takes a deep breath like he's fighting for composure, and I let my gaze skate lower. The way his jeans are unbuttoned, I can see that happy trail of hair beneath his belly button before it disappears further down. The sight has me strangely aware of my body, of the way my cold nipples are straining against the fabric of my dress.

"I've had enough of this," he grumps. He yanks a phone from the pocket of his jeans. One arm moves easily and freely. It's the one he uses to tap the screen.

I take a step closer and peer over his shoulder. Or I try to. I'm much too short to manage looking over a giant's shoulder, so I end up peering around his beefy arm instead. He's so big, solid, and warm.

"Ha! I was right, real country!" I say in a singsong voice.

He yanks the phone out of my view. "And what's the population?"

"Twenty-six thousand, four hundred, and twelve. Last census two years ago," I answer easily. I've spent my life being briefed on every minute detail of my country. I can stand a pop quiz from a stranger. Especially an American one.

"And the primary crop?"

"Wheat and barley. Though most of the farming done is livestock farming due to our mountainous terrain." Velkan is a small coastal country with a long and distinguished history. We've fought for our freedom and though there's much poverty, we are a proud people.

He snorts. "You could have studied up on the country."

I roll my eyes. He's being so obtuse. "You could look up a picture of the princess."

He taps hurriedly at the screen and looks between the phone and me. "You could have dyed your hair. And where's your entourage? Wouldn't royalty travel with bodyguards? This is not making sense."

"It makes perfect sense. You're my prince, and I've come to take you back to Velkan. Didn't you listen to *any* of my messages?" I huff out and start moving around the cabin. I need to get dry, and I'll be in a much better mood.

"Where are you going?" He follows me through the hallway. "I have nothing valuable for you to make off with."

"I want a fucking towel," I tell him, and the moment the dirty word leaves my mouth, I clap my hand over it. I spend too much time in the public eye to make a habit of cursing. To swear invites criticism of the crown.

But Rafael chuckles as he looks me up and down. He seems to realize that I might be cold. He tips his head in a gesture for me to follow him and leads me to the bathroom. It's a huge, sprawling one complete with a hot tub in the corner. I gaze longingly at it. I'd give anything for a good soak, but there's no time for that.

Right now, my mission is to convince my prince to return with me so we can marry and rule together. The prince doesn't even seem to know he's a prince. The thought makes me sad for him. He has no clue of his history, no idea of his people.

He passes me a towel. Our fingertips brush, and I suck in a breath at the electricity that arcs between us. I've never had that reaction to a man before. I thought it was the stuff in those silly rom-coms I watch late at night when I can't sleep.

"So, if you're from Vulcan..."

"Velkan," I correct again as I undo my soggy ponytail and wring it out in the towel.

He watches me intently, some emotion I can't describe flickering across his face. Is it longing? Loneliness, perhaps. "Then where is your magical prince from?"

"The neighboring Republic of Portia."

"Ahh, of course."

"You've heard of it?" A little bit of hope flutters in my heart. Maybe he can explain to me how he ended up here in the States where he grew up instead of with his family. The little information I managed to gather seems to suggest that most in the kingdom have no idea that Rafael is alive and well.

"Nope," he calls over his shoulder as he retreats from the bathroom. He returns thirty seconds later with a t-shirt and boxers. He shoves them at me with a grunt. "You'll catch your death of a cold."

He gestures for me to change and turns his back to me.

I peel off my sticky clothes, using the towel to pat dry my skin and clean the mud from my feet. "When were you sent to America? It's a weird place. They have no concept of personal space here. They bump right into you. I had the rudest woman next to me on the plane. Even spilled her peanuts on my lap."

"Tell me again why you think I'm a prince," he demands. He certainly has that air of authority that accompanies those who are royalty.

I glance at the clothes he gave me and decide that no matter what's proper, I'm not wearing wet panties to bed. I shed my undergarments, adding them to the pile of wet clothes at my feet and tug on his black t-shirt. It's more like a dress given that he's a giant, and I'm a short girl. I don't bother with the boxers. It would feel too intimate.

"I don't think you're a prince. I *know* you're one." Violet personally reviewed the information. She's always thorough, and she's never led me wrong. "You can turn around now."

"This is getting ridiculous. Tell you what. I'll let you stay the night then tomorrow morning, we'll get you a ride share. Hell, I'll spring for it. And you'll leave my mountain and never return." He nods to himself as if the matter is settled.

I have no intention of leaving without the grumpy mountain man. He is my groom, and the sooner he accepts the fact, the faster we can be wed. But it's late, and I'm tired. I'll argue with the cranky giant tomorrow. "Very well. You may show me to my quarters."

4
RAFE

"You didn't have to make her sleep on the lumpy couch, asshole." I stare up at the exposed wood beams. I built this place after traveling around the country. The cabin is supposed to be my oasis, but it's hard to be peaceful when I can feel her presence. I can sense her shifting on the couch and hear each soft sigh as she attempts to get comfortable.

"This is ridiculous," I mutter as I reach for my phone. I know damn well she's not a princess even if she does happen to bear a striking resemblance to the woman from Velkan, which still doesn't sound like a real country to me.

Roman answers on the first ring. "You remember my scammer?"

He grunts, and I realize that it's past midnight. I

should apologize, but I need this resolved. I need to know she's a liar so I can stop thinking about her pert breasts heaving beneath my t-shirt, about how seeing her in my clothes made me want to pound on my chest like some caveman. "She's here."

"Fuck." Roman finally sounds awake. "Do you have a gun with you?"

"She's not a threat," I scoff. Unless he counts her as a threat to my sanity because I nearly lost my mind when I saw those perfect, creamy thighs peeking out from under my t-shirt. Never wanted to drop to my knees. Never wanted to spread a woman and discover all of her secret places. She's fucking with my brain, that's why I have to get Roman to remind me she's a liar.

With a deep breath, I quickly recap the situation. He'll know how to track down information. He spent years in prison before building a reputable construction business which means he has an endless list of contacts on both sides of the law.

"And you don't remember anything before age five?" Roman repeats, clinging to that detail for some reason.

I push back the image of a woman with dark hair, one who spoke kindly to me and read bedtime stories. *She's not real.* I have to remind myself of that.

She's a figment of my imagination, a memory a little boy manufactured to make himself feel safe while growing up in the system.

My voice wavers, "Nothing relevant."

"Anything you can tell me might be helpful in getting the answers faster."

The orange glow that haunts my dreams flashes in my mind, but I push against it too. That's a nightmare. I must have seen something scary on TV when I was young. "Find what you can."

No one else has ever been able to answer questions about my past. When I was young, the center holding my records was damaged in a tornado, and most of the records were lost. Back then, everything was still on paper, so no digital copies exist of who I am.

"This could open up some things that you don't want to know," Roman warns like I haven't already considered that possibility a dozen times before. But it's time to face this and figure out who I am.

He sighs, and I hear the soft shuffle of feet against carpet. He must be away on a job, staying overnight at a hotel. He does that sometimes. "What does she want from you?"

"She wants to marry me." The thought is laughable. I've never had a family. I bounced around the system for years without finding a permanent home. I figure that was a good thing. I learned early on in life that people leave me behind.

He smothers a snort. "She pretty?"

An irrational surge of anger floods my veins. "What the fuck does it matter to you?"

He barks out a laugh. "I'll take that as a yes. Listen, she figured out you have some zeroes in the bank and wants a piece of the action. That's all this is."

When I aged out of the system, all I had was the t-shirt on my back and a few scant toiletries tucked away in a garbage bag. I spent time on the streets until I bought a winning lottery ticket. I claimed the jackpot anonymously and spent the next few years traveling the country in an RV with all the amenities.

Somehow though, my identity must have been compromised. It's the only thing that makes sense. I grip the phone tighter, hating the thought. "Check into her."

"I'll turn over every rock," he promises before we disconnect the call.

After that, I try to settle back into my bed and sleep. But instead, I spend the night restless, wondering about the curvy woman on my couch. She can't really be a princess because I'm no prince.

THE NEXT MORNING, I'M IN THE KITCHEN SIPPING ONE of my overpriced coffees. Coffee is one of my few addictions. Despite my simple way of living, I still find myself going into town to purchase these special little pods.

I spent an uneasy night in my bed. For the few minutes I did manage to sleep, the orange glow was back. But it was different this time. There wasn't just orange. There was a strange man, a figure cloaked in darkness. He came for me, beckoned me close.

When I got up, I shook off the dream and took a long shower. During it, I decided to let this girl stick around for a couple of days until Roman figures out what's going on. For some reason, I feel protective over her. Like she's mine to look after.

Once Roman brings me evidence that she's a con artist, I'll get her the help she needs. Then I can go back to my quiet life.

Aurora rises from the couch and stumbles into the kitchen. Her hair is matted and plastered to her head. Dark circles are under her eyes as though she didn't sleep at all. I feel a stab of guilt for that. I could have given her the bed. See, further proof I'm no prince. A real prince would have given her the bed.

"You snore," she hisses instead of greeting me.

"Herbert has never complained," I counter, not sure why I find her so damn adorable like this. What would it be like to have a woman around, someone to spend my days annoying?

"And who is Herbert? Because he must be deaf!"

"My turtle."

She whirls around and pins me with a look that tells me she does not find this amusing.

I fight a grin and jerk my head toward the coffee machine. "Want some?"

She moves to stand in front of it then she freezes as though she has no clue what she's doing. She blinks up at me with her big doe eyes and my gaze goes to her puffy, pink lips. What would they feel like under mine? Fuck, I should not be thinking that when she's here to deceive me and take my money.

The slightest ring of vulnerability is in her tone when she says, "Can you show me how? I have people to do this for me."

"Of course, you do," I mutter under my breath as I reach for the machine. It's not meant to come out as grumpy as it does. Then again, I've never been a people person. There's a reason I only have Herbert for company.

I show her how to load the machine and point to the buttons. "Choose your size."

She studies the buttons for so long it's almost comical.

"Go with the medium." I will not let her innocent behavior make me think she's really a princess. I won't let the way my t-shirt dips low on her chest make me wonder about the exact shade of her nipples.

She presses the button. When the coffee begins brewing, she claps her hands together in delight and graces me with the biggest smile I've ever seen.

"I made coffee for myself!" She says this as though she's never done it in her life. For a moment, a flicker of doubt goes through me. Is it possible she is who she claims to be?

"Thank you." She reaches around me for her mug. Except that my brain gets it all scrambled and thinks for some crazy reason that she's going in for a kiss.

I drop my head, suddenly aware of the way our breaths mingle, of the way her eyes are so big and round. But most of all, I'm aware of how her breasts are pushing against my chest. They're rounded and heavy, and my fingers itch to reach out and squeeze them.

She whimpers, the slightest sound of desire, and it's enough to pull me from my trance. It doesn't matter if she's a con artist or a princess. I'm not kissing her, and I'm definitely not falling in love with her.

Aurora

I THOUGHT HE WAS GOING TO KISS ME, AND I'M surprised by how disappointed I am when Rafael pulls back.

He moves to the fridge, muttering something under his breath. He pulls out plastic bottles. I'm not even sure what they are, but he must have a dozen of them.

"Flavorings," he grunts out the word.

I wait, confused by his bottles and his almost kiss. He has beautiful thick lips. The kind that I can't help wanting to run my tongue across.

"They're for the coffee. You pour them in to give it a gourmet flavor."

I think I understand now. I scan a few of the bottles, selecting a caramel one. I add a liberal amount of it to my cup. Wanting to break the tension in the air, I say, "Tell me about Herbert."

"He's the closest thing I have to a pet, I guess."

I think longingly of my horse, Moxie, and the way she's comforted me since my mom's death. Sometimes, pets understand us on a level no one else does. I make a mental note that we'll need travel arrangements for his turtle. It wouldn't be right for Rafael to leave him behind.

I look around the cabin, also noting that my husband-to-be doesn't have a lot in the way of material possessions. The whole cabin is rustic and simple though spacious. The vaulted ceilings and large windows give it an airy feeling. It's a far cry from Father's castle with its five dining halls and endless sitting rooms all filled with ornate treasures designed to remind visitors of our status. "What do you normally do in the mornings?"

"Check on my crops. I'm not much of a farmer, just believe in living off the land. I grow most of my own food, and I trade with some of the other mountain men for things like meat."

He's independent and rugged. Will he like living in the castle where there are people to do even the most basic tasks for him? Or will he grow bored and resent me for bringing him into so much splendor?

"You could help me for the day...if you don't have

any royal duties to attend to." There's a definite note of sarcasm in his voice. He still doesn't believe I am who I say I am.

I've never been one to back down from a fight, so I hold my head high and meet his gaze confidently. "I'd love to."

5

AURORA

"CAN I MEET HERBERT?" I ASK AFTER I'VE FINISHED
the tour of Rafael's gardens. He spent the morning
showing me his crops. He seemed to think I would
be disgusted by the dirt and the worms and the hard
work. But I spent the day shoulder-to-shoulder with
him, doing the same tasks. I want my mountain man
to know I'm interested in more than a marriage in
name. I want to be partners in every sense of the
word, and that means pulling my weight.

Besides, I know Rafael's secret now. He might
march around here like a big grump, scowling at me.
But the man talks to his tomato plants. He fusses
over his cucumbers, turning them to make sure
they're getting enough sunlight then he bends low to

speak words of encouragement over the lettuce heads he's growing.

He struggles to move sometimes. I see the way his balance is affected, the way he can't control his limb movements. I've always taken for granted the fact that if I tell my body to pick up a shovel, it will. If I tell my fingers to release the handle of the hose, they will. But his muscles don't work the same way.

"Sure, but I have to warn you, turtles are the ultimate introverts." I think he made a joke. I'm finding that I like Rafael's dry sense of humor. He makes a quiet joke, but he never draws attention to it.

Rafael leads me to the backyard where he shows me the enclosure he's built. Carefully, he pulls back the netting, pausing to explain, "He's a Carolina box turtle."

I look down to see a turtle plodding along the grass with a yellow and brown pattern on his back. He's kind of cute with his long neck and dark eyes. "Can I touch him?"

He nods. "Gently. The same way you can feel it when someone presses on your fingernail, he can feel it when you touch his shell. And don't try to pick him up. He doesn't like that."

When Rafael has finished with his instructions, I

reach out and touch the shell. It's hard and cold beneath my fingertips, reminding me of a stone.

Herbert blinks up at me, seemingly unaffected by my presence.

"He's lovely. What happened to his shell?" There's a jagged line bisecting it.

"Not sure. Probably a bird picked him up and dropped him. I found the little guy on the side of the road and managed to get him back into good health. But he's no longer strong enough to be on his own."

"You found him on the side of the road," I say softly, my attention snagged on that detail.

"He was alone like me," Rafe says and immediately ducks his head as if he didn't mean to reveal that detail about himself.

My heart hurts for this mountain man. While he snored last night, I searched through the cabin for clues about him. I couldn't find family pictures or photo albums. Nothing to tell me who Rafael is or where he comes from. It made me sad for him.

I've grown up in a kingdom where my ancestors' portraits hang on the walls. I've spent my life being taught about my history, my lineage, where I come from. I know who I am. I know who those were before me. I feel their presence and carry them with me.

"Time for lunch," he says right as my stomach growls.

We start the walk back to his place, and I follow him. I'm dirty, sweaty, and completely invigorated by today's work. I'm not sure how much land he owns on this mountain, but it seems like a lot. My fingers itch to spend a day painting the breathtaking landscape onto a canvas. "This is beautiful. I get why you love living here."

"It's my first real home. As a boy, I grew up in the foster system. Bounced around from place to place. I never knew how long I'd get to stay or where I was going next."

He grew up in the foster system. It makes sense why he has no personal photos, but if he's really who Violet claims he is, why did he end up here? Why didn't the Republic of Portia claim him? I doubt he knows the answers to those questions any more than I do.

"So, what made you pick Courage?" I called Violet last night after I went through Rafael's things. I reassured her that I was fine and that Rafael was being a wonderful host. I didn't want her to worry or think I can't do this.

"Just drove in here one day, and it felt right.

Someone told me that Courage is the place where every outcast finds home." His phone rings, and he pauses so abruptly that I bump into his sweaty, t-shirt clad back. He's so solid, so warm against my cheek.

Quickly, I straighten as he murmurs a curse under his breath. He answers his call but doesn't move away from me. I can hear another deep voice on the other end. "Everything checks out. Aurora is a princess, and she snuck away to the States to find her prince."

My heart pounds. He had someone checking into me. Does that mean that everyone knows I'm gone? How did his contact get this information?

"Do you want me to keep looking into your background?"

Rafael sighs deeply, and I wonder if he's disappointed. "You won't find anything but yeah, go for it."

He ends the call without another word while I hold my breath. I don't know what to say, and we stand for long moments. The silence is broken by the love songs from happy birds and the low drone of bees buzzing nearby.

Finally, he lets out a chuckle. "You're royalty."

Does this mean he's going to treat me differently

now? Will he become somber and stiff around me, like everyone else except for Violet?

"Yeah." It's the most undignified word I've ever said in my life. A princess doesn't use casual slang, but I don't care as I kick at the dirt with the toe of the too-big boot that Rafael loaned me.

He turns to me. Sadness flickers across his features. "I'm not who you think I am."

I don't bother arguing with him. If his contact was able to discover that I'm the princess, then he'll soon have confirmation that he's the prince. Will he shirk his duty once he knows? No, I can't let him. I have to convince him that we're meant to be before then.

"So, what am I supposed to do with you, princess?" He glances away from me, and it almost sounds like he's asking himself the question.

Still, I answer. "You could start by feeding me."

He nods. "Come on then. I'll school you in the culinary art of peanut butter and jelly."

───────

"AND THIS IS A DELICACY IN YOUR COUNTRY?" I ASK AS I watch Rafael move around his kitchen, placing various items on the island.

"The best," he insists, adding a jar of peanut butter to the counter.

I tap the bright orange lid. "I've never been allowed to eat junk food. I've heard Americans are obsessed with it."

"Well, not only are you eating junk food, today, you'll learn how to make it." He produces a rolling pin like I've seen the chefs use in our kitchens.

A wave of excitement rolls through me. I've always wanted to learn the basics of cooking. Now it looks like I'm going to get a chance.

"You make your own bread?" I ask in awe as he produces a loaf of bread. It's homemade and light golden brown, like something out of a magazine spread.

The slightest pink tinge starts beneath his beard as he ducks his head. "Anyone can do this."

"Is the peanut butter homemade too?"

"Store bought is best in these cases." He slides me a kitchen knife. "Cut four slices."

I hesitate. He didn't make fun of me for not knowing how to make coffee earlier. Still, I hate looking helpless in front of Rafael.

He makes a soft sound. "They really didn't let you do anything."

I wait for him to laugh at me or make fun of the

fact that I have no real-world skills. But he doesn't. He moves to stand behind me, so close I can feel the heat from his body. Something electric crackles between us. If he feels it too, he ignores it.

He places the kitchen knife in my hand, showing me how to hold it. He guides it, putting his big, work-roughened hands over mine. "Like this."

I lean back against him, seeking his warmth. I press my back to his front and the rightness of the posture makes a contented hum come from my throat.

But I don't think Rafael likes it because he growls. It's a low, menacing sound that a predator would make. Before I can analyze it, he steps away from me.

Rejection stings, causing my cheeks to heat. I clear my throat and try to get us back on solid ground. I try to think of something that might be a safe topic. "Who taught you how to cook?"

Behind me, Rafe swallows hard. For a moment I don't think he's going to answer, then he explains, "One of my foster moms."

"Were you close to her?"

He says nothing.

I want to ask a million questions, but I don't.

Maybe in time my future husband will open up to me. Maybe in time, he'll trust me with his secrets.

"It's time to roll the bread."

For this task, he hands me the rolling pin. "Get it as flat as possible."

Even though he stepped away a moment ago, he once again covers my hands with his. Another flare of attraction goes through me. Does he feel this, too? Does he feel the same zing of awareness?

He hands me another knife when we're done. "Now apply the peanut butter with even strokes."

I glance at his face, attempting to read his emotions. Something in his expression makes me think he's not as unaffected by my presence as he likes to pretend. He likes me too. But for some reason, he's holding himself back. Does it have to do with the fact that I'm the princess? Or is it because he's unwilling to leave this life he's built for himself of rugged independence?

I'm afraid to ask these questions out loud and drive him further away. So instead, I listen to his instructions and follow along until we have very flat sandwiches.

"Now what?" They're flat blobs of bread with peanut butter and jelly on them. There's no way to pick them up.

"Now, we close them and fry them." He shows me how to close the sandwich and heats oil in a frying pan. "Everyone should know how to fry a sandwich. It's one of life's little pleasures."

"And this will taste good?" I ask again as I put my sandwich in the pan. He's still standing so close to me and yet he's not touching me. The distance between us feels like a chasm that I desperately want to close.

As soon as the sandwiches are cooked, he shows me how to dust them with powdered sugar before we take them to the back porch. We sit side by side on the steps.

I bite into mine and barely contain a groan. The warm peanut butter is gooey and perfectly mixes with the grape jam. The sweet, crusty outside has the perfect amount of crunch. "This is so good."

I look up to see Rafe watching me chew and for a moment, I'm worried I have something on my face. But then he looks away and takes a bite of his own food. "My foster mom taught me how to make these. She was...number seven, I think. Anyway, she was my favorite. Never got mad at me for not knowing how to do stuff that regular people already know."

"Like cooking," I say softly, the pieces falling into place. Maybe Rafael and I aren't so different. He was deprived of learning about the world in a different way. While I was intentionally sheltered, he was never taught by a caring adult. "Do you still talk to her?"

He shakes his head. "No, uh, they had three biological sons. One of them got sick and well, it was expensive, so they had to cut costs somewhere."

"I don't follow."

He swallows the rest of his sandwich in one big bite. "They sent me back to social services. One less mouth to feed. Plus, you know physical therapy isn't cheap."

"Physical therapy?" I think my mom had that after a horse-riding accident when I was young. I thought it was something only injured people do.

"For cerebral palsy," he explains. "It's why my body...doesn't. Why I don't move easy and can't always relax some muscles. It's a movement disorder."

"But you don't have a wheelchair," I say and immediately blush. "It's just that I've seen people with it on the internet. They're usually a lot worse than you. I mean, it's not a competition...oh, I'm messing this up. I want to be supportive and say the right things, and I don't know what they are."

Half his mouth tips up in an almost smile. "Like a

lot of conditions, it exists on a spectrum. One person might be severely affected to the point of being permanently disabled. Another person may only be affected mildly, to the point that they can be perceived as healthy."

"Is it painful?"

"Yeah, the muscle pain when your body twists up is pretty bad. But the stares in public are worse. The pity, the curiosity. You want to go to the fuckin' grocery store without people staring and acting like you're a circus act."

My heart twists at what he's saying. "You're not serious."

He watches a squirrel.

"You haven't had an easy life," I say the realization creeping over me. I don't know why it makes my heart hurt to imagine that Rafael's life has been so difficult. I barely know the guy, and yet I want to hug away his pain.

"You haven't had an easy life either, princess."

My eyes widen. I think he's the first person to ever say that to me. Most people assume because I've grown up in splendor that I've been allowed to do whatever I want.

"I'm scared to go back. Being here with you is the first taste of freedom that I've had. In my whole life,

I've never gotten to be free. I've always felt…caged." Admitting those words out loud is the scariest thing I've done in a long time.

Some emotion I can't define flickers across his face. "We'll make the most of it. What are some normal, everyday activities that you've always wanted to try?

I take another bite of my gooey sandwich. "Well, cooking for one. Gardening, camping. Ooh, I've always wanted to try camping."

When Rafael looks at me, his eyes are smiling. "One camping trip coming right up."

6

RAFE

ONE HOUR LATER, I'M STANDING IN GRIZZ'S OUTDOOR shop, trying to pretend I know what the hell I'm doing.

"This is so exciting," Aurora gushes for the third time in as many minutes. "I had no idea you were such an outdoorsman."

I'm outdoorsy in that I know how to grow vegetables. I know fuck all about camping, but the hero worship in Aurora's gaze is doing something funny to my insides. It's making me want to be worthy of that look. "Love the outdoors. Can't get enough of them."

"I bet you've been camping a million times," she says and turns to the display of tents. "In your expert opinion, which one would be the best?"

I chance a look at Grizz who's standing a few feet from us. He's been quietly eavesdropping since we came into the shop. He offered to help us, but Aurora waved him off.

Grizz subtly gestures to the one on the top shelf, careful not to attract Aurora's attention. I owe the man a steak for having my back. So far, he's quietly directed us to the best hiking boots and ponchos for the adventure.

"This one," I yank it from the shelf. "It's weather-proof which is great for the uh, weather."

She frowns. "Are we expecting bad weather tonight?"

"Never can be too careful," I answer, as if I thought to check out the forecast for tonight. In truth, I saw the look of hope in Aurora's eyes when she said she wanted to go camping. In that moment, I decided she'd get to experience this at least once in her life.

Grizz makes a motion like he's swatting away bugs.

I clear my throat and add, "Also the netting does...repels mosquitoes."

"That sounds good to me," she answers and follows me up to the counter where Grizz has been carefully stacking our purchases. I see he's added a few extra things, battery powered lanterns and other items I wouldn't have thought to include.

While Aurora goes to the restroom, I pay for the purchase.

"You know where your property ends and Roman's begins?" He asks.

I nod. I'm familiar with the boundary lines on these mountains though they're rarely enforced. As long as we all respect each other's properties, no one has any issues. I've always lived peaceably with my fellow mountain men.

"There's a clearing with a lake and a fire pit. Set your tent about fifteen feet away from both of those. Avoid putting it under the trees, and don't keep food out."

I yank out my credit card and pass it to him. "Your next beer at Liquid Courage is on me."

He chuckles as he bags up the order. "Invite me to the wedding."

We arrive at the spot Grizz mentioned by late afternoon. Storm clouds are already gathering overhead.

"Should we go back?" Aurora asks.

Thunder cracks, but I think about how this might be her one and only chance to experience everyday things like this. "What's a little bit of water?"

The smile she gives me tells me that I made the right call. She wants this camping trip as much as I do, and I won't stand in the way of her dreams.

"What's the first step?" She looks at me expectantly.

"Choose a place to put down the tent. Anywhere with flat ground is perfect. We want to avoid tree roots and rocks." Yeah, that sounds smart. That sounds like I know what I'm doing.

She begins walking the perimeter of the clearing, studying the ground beneath her new hiking boots with the bright pink laces. She squealed when she saw them, and I knew right then they were going in the cart.

It's funny how two days ago we were perfect strangers, and now I'd do anything to make her smile. Because when she smiles everything in my world feels right. Something that's been tight in my chest eases, and I can breathe.

She selects a spot, and points in the distance. "This is perfect. See that? We have a view of the sunflower field you planted." Her expression wavers, a frown marring her features. "My parents were married for over twenty years. My dad never brought my mom flowers, never tried to do nice things to make her smile. I mean, she was always doing things for him. But I don't think he ever noticed."

My heart twists in my chest. "Sunflowers are your favorite, huh?"

She beams up at me, the frown fading. It strikes me then that she hasn't had a lot of people listen to her. Not really *listen*. "They're bright and sunshiny, and they stand tall. They're proud of who they are."

I nod as we begin to spread out the ground sheet. Next is the tent and there are plenty of pieces that would be unfamiliar to me. Except that Grizz had my back and already explained exactly how to set this up, so I don't look dumb in front of my girl.

We finish as light rain starts, and we take shelter in our newly formed tent complete with top of the line sleeping bags.

Aurora settles on top of her bag, crossing her legs. The motion causes those little hiking shorts she bought at the store to ride even higher. If I ever needed proof there is a higher power, it's right here in this tent with Aurora's sweet scent filling the space and her tiny shorts tempting me. I'd love nothing more than to yank them down, put her on all fours, and take her from behind.

She's oblivious to the filthy movie playing in my mind as she searches the backpack for the protein bars. "I'm really glad you thought of these since it doesn't look like we'll be getting a real dinner over the fire. Do you think the tent will hold?"

I sit down gingerly, thankful that her attention is still captivated by the contents of the bag. Otherwise, she'd see the monster bulge between my legs and probably take off running.

"Don't know. My first camping trip." As soon as the words are out of my mouth, I regret them. I'm no prince, but I can take care of her.

Her mouth hangs open for a split second then she throws her head back and laughs. "This is your first camping trip. Why didn't you tell me?"

I shrug, not sure if I should tell her the truth. But then I decide to go for it. "I wanted everything to be perfect for you for one day."

Her smile softens and she scoots closer to me. Something electric arcs between us. Something that has nothing to do with the thunderstorm. Rain is dripping down onto the tent outside, creating a gentle soundtrack.

She's looking at me with hero worship, so close our breaths mingle. When she tilts her head toward mine, I meet her the rest of the way. Our lips are crashing against each other. My arms go around her body, and I pull her into my lap. Heaven, I've found heaven.

When she moans against my mouth, I use the moment to slip my tongue inside. Slowly, I stroke her, learning all the places that make her arch against me, fusing our bodies together.

She breaks the kiss long enough to gulp down oxygen but even as she does, she's fisting the material of my t-shirt even tighter. Her eyes are dilated, pupils blown. Every desperate gasp for oxygen pushes her tits higher, and I have to see her naked. Have to taste every inch of her skin.

"I want to lick your pretty pussy." It's not exactly a romantic movie moment. It's a crude confession, but I can't keep it inside any longer. I've wondered what she'll taste like since the moment she arrived on my doorstep.

She shivers in my arms, her pointed nipples grazing against my t-shirt. I could come right here with her in my arms. It wouldn't take much to set me off, but I want to make this good for her. I have a feeling this curvy princess is as untouched and inexperienced as I am. And if I'm going to be her first, I'll damn sure make it good for her.

"I want that too." Her words are a breathy whimper.

I'm glad I insisted now on getting the tent all set up. Even the pillows have been inflated, which is a good damn thing because I'm too wired to think about doing anything else right now. Animal need courses through my veins, something primal in me rising up and demanding that I fuck my woman. "Lean back."

I reach for the hem of her shirt next. I need to see her tits, need to see all of her hills and valleys. By the time I'm done, there won't be a place on her body that she hasn't been well-loved.

She puts her hands over mine, stilling me. "Um, this is my first time. I mean, it's not a terribly big deal. I haven't been saving myself or anything like that. I've been too carefully supervised to be allowed to do anything with a boy and now, I'm here with you and try not to be too disappointed. I probably won't be very good at it."

Her cheeks are dark pink by the time she finishes speaking, and my heart is long gone. It's hers now. I'm pretty sure I lost it the moment she showed up on my porch.

I take her face in my hands. "It's OK. We'll learn together."

A slow smile spreads across her face as understanding dawns. "It's your first time too."

I make a little hum of acknowledgement as I press my lips against hers again, tasting her sweet flavor. I always thought that if I were lucky enough to find a woman, I'd be humiliated about my lack of experience. Never thought I'd be grateful for it, thankful that I waited until I found the woman I want to put my kid into.

I move to press kisses along her jaw, around her ear, and down the column of her throat. She makes small whimpers under her breath, turning her head so I can have better access, and I smile against her skin. "Gonna take your clothes off now."

This time she lets me pull her t-shirt over her head and instantly my gaze goes to the pink bra she's wearing. It's lacy and pushes her tits up.

Slowly, I reach for the strap and pull it down, pausing to kiss her shoulder. Even though my cock is demanding that I hurry this along, I ignore him. This is about making her feel safe, precious, and treasured. So, I unwrap her slowly, pulling off her clothes and kissing her flushed skin until she's stretched out, looking up at me with so much trust that it damn near guts me. I will always be worthy of that look from her, always fight for her, and always love her.

I spend long minutes exploring her body, sucking

on her tits, and licking my way down her rounded belly. I knead her flesh, murmuring words of appreciation for her beautiful curves. She's sharing them with me, giving me the gift of her body.

When I get to her panty-clad mound, I inhale deeply. Her aroma is intoxicating, and my mouth is watering already.

Aurora is on her elbows, looking down at me with a glassy gaze. She gives me the slightest nod, and I reach for her wet panties. I remove them slowly, pulling them over her ankles.

She parts her thighs for me, and the sight of those soaked curls makes my cock even harder. I reach down and squeeze the fucker. My come is now hers. It belongs in her body.

Dipping my head, I nuzzle the inside of her thighs. Fuck, the smell of her wet pussy is my new favorite scent. Gonna get it all on my face and in my beard. Gonna wear it like cologne so any bastard who comes near her knows that I'm the man who satisfies her.

She giggles and when I look up at her, she offers softly, "Your beard tickles."

"That's not the only thing it can do," I growl as I spread her pussy lips with my fingers. Fuck, all that pink perfection is mine. She belongs to me now, and

I'll be the man who lives on his knees to please his princess.

I lick a broad stripe along her seam.

Instantly, her thighs go around my ears, squeezing me tight. But it's not enough to mute the sounds of her pleasure.

I eat her out, licking her until she's tugging on my hair so hard my scalp stings. She screams when the thunder booms, and it's when she completely relaxes that I start again. This time, I pin her hips down and wedge my shoulders between her thighs. Then I work my fingers into her tight little opening while sucking her bud into my mouth.

Between her thighs is my new favorite place I decide as she shatters again, flooding my fingers with more moisture. She's so damn wet and tight. I don't know how I'll ever work my big cock into her.

She whimpers as the release ends, and I kiss my way back up her body. I push her hair from her sweaty forehead. She's my forever, and one day soon, she'll realize I'm not the prince she's been looking for.

7

AURORA

"You're scowling," I murmur as I lie completely naked on top of my sleeping bag. The tent is muggy. The air inside thick with the scent of our arousal, but I don't care at this moment. All that matters is becoming one with my grumpy mountain man. As soon as I can feel my legs again.

I raise my hand to ease the wrinkles on his forehead. I don't know why I like it so much when he scowls, but I do. It makes him look extra grumpy.

"What's wrong?" I ask, deciding that it must be me. Maybe he didn't like what we did, but that can't be right. Not if that bulge between his legs is any indication. I think maybe eating my pussy turned him on as much as it turned me on.

"I'm no prince," he says in a rush. Like he's

forcing the words out from a throat that's too tight. "Do you still want this?"

I smile at him, my heart overflowing with love. It's too soon to tell him. We've barely known each other for two days. Still, I know in my heart that Rafael is my prince. He's my soulmate. But I think that something in his past must have convinced him he's not enough. It hurts my heart to think of a little boy sent back to an orphanage after he thought he'd found his forever family.

"It wouldn't matter to me if you were a beggar on the streets. I'd still want this." I don't want there to be any doubt in his mind. I let my hand drift to his belt and give it a tug.

He lets me help him out of his clothes then we're naked in the tent together. Neither of us moves for a moment. We stare at each other's bodies. His is all hard lines and sharp angles while mine is soft curves and rounded edges. Yet somehow, we'll fit together.

He pumps his shaft and stares down at me with so much longing written on his face. "I'll go slow. If it's too much, tell me. I'll find a way—fuck, I'll find a way to stop."

"Get inside me," I pant, spreading my legs even more for him.

I've never wanted anyone this way. Sure, I've read

romance books, and I've watched rom-coms, but I never understood the desperate need. The primal urge to have someone until Rafael with his scowling looks and his big body and the way he makes me feel so protected and safe. Even now with the rain dripping down on the tent, all I can think about is how he didn't know a thing about camping, but he still wanted to make sure I had a good time.

Rafael rolls over me. Instead of immediately pushing into me, he grinds our bodies together. His cock nudges at my swollen folds while he kisses my neck. He sucks and nibbles until more moisture is dripping from me and I'm pleading with him to push inside of me.

He lines up our bodies and shoves his broad head inside. The stretch burns at first but slowly eases.

When he reaches for my clit, he circles it gently with his thumb. He's saying things to me. But I'm not sure what he's saying because I'm already lost in a haze of pleasure having been primed from the previous two orgasms.

The glassy look in Rafe's eyes tells me that he's as far gone as I am.

When he pushes through my virgin barrier, there's a moment of pain but he instantly stills himself and presses little kisses to my forehead. He's murmuring something again, calling me his good girl. He's reassuring me that it will feel good in a minute, that he'll always be the man to satisfy me and take care of my urges.

When the pain recedes, I open my eyes and let out a breath, sinking into the moment with him.

He's been holding himself so still. There's sweat on his forehead making his hair stick to his face. When I give him a nod, his control snaps. He pulls all the way out only to thrust quickly inside again.

He feels so good. For the first time in a long time, I feel happy, complete, and safe because I'm right here with him. With Rafael who will protect me from the world. Rafael who wants to give me everything he can. Rafael who makes my heart pound and my mouth go dry.

"Come for me," he murmurs softly when I clench around him. The orgasm barrels down on me, and I rake my nails along his back. It makes him move faster, makes every thrust deeper.

I come in a blinding rush of white-hot light, a flame consuming my body. As I float back down, I feel his release start too. His come is shooting deep into my body. It's then I realize Rafe isn't just the man I want ruling beside me on the throne. He's the man I want to be my husband and the father of my children.

"Are you alright?" He asks, his voice tinged with a note of panic.

I blink and realize he's watery. I sniff and manage weakly, "I'm great."

I mean it, too. I didn't expect to fall in love with this man. And now that I have, I can't help but worry about what happens when he finds out he's a real prince. He's so against the idea, and I'm afraid he'll never leave this mountain and join me in the kingdom. But there's no way for me to leave my country behind. Not when so many people are depending on me.

"I'm happy," I manage to tell him.

He eases out of my body and collapses next to me on the tent floor. He pulls me until I'm lying over his chest and rubs my back. "Did I hurt you?"

I shake my head against his chest even as more tears come. He's so sweet and gentle and tender. I want us to be together forever. But I'm not sure that's going to happen.

I don't want to put that kind of pressure on him or freak him out. Instead, I tell him the truth. "I didn't expect all of this, how intense it was."

He continues to rub my back. "Cry it out if you

need to. I've got you."

His words warm the part of me that's felt alone since I lost my mom. "You're the first person that's held me since my mom passed away, and I miss her every day."

Lying here with him and thinking about a future together is making me think of all the moments that she won't be there. Like when I get married or when I have my first baby or when I'm crowned queen. She won't be there to see any of that stuff. She'll never get to meet Rafael or know how incredibly happy he makes me.

"When did you lose her?"

"When I was thirteen. Sometimes, I can't believe that it's been so long. It doesn't feel that way. It feels like I was talking to her yesterday and today, I woke up and she's not there anymore."

He makes a consoling noise. It's a soft rumble that I feel through his chest into mine.

I look up at him, seeing all the pity and sorrow in his gaze. "I wish she could meet you."

"She already has. She's looking down from Heaven and watching over you, which means she watched you stumble into my cabin and march around like you own the place."

I chuckle. How could that have been yesterday?

How could this man now feel like an essential part of my heart, like the part of me that I'll never be able to let go?

"Do you remember your mom?" I ask, my voice hesitant. I'm afraid to broach the subject for fear of pushing at old wounds. There's still so much I want to know about this mountain man, and I only have a week to convince him to come back with me.

He's quiet for so long that I don't think he's going to answer the question. Then he says, "I don't really remember anything before five. Sometimes, I don't know if that's bad or good."

"So, you have no memories of your mom." Even if she did pass away, he should remember something before he was five. It's strange that he can't.

He hesitates before admitting, "Sometimes in my mind's eye, I see a woman with dark hair and gray eyes. She's hugging me and telling me she loves me and reading bedtime stories."

"Do you think that's her?" I wonder if I could find her for him. The palace has plenty of resources, and Violet has connections everywhere. She could help me.

"I think that was a scared little boy's way of coping with the fact that he was an orphan," he answers, his voice dejected.

"What if it wasn't? What if that's really a memory of her?"

His expression falls and I know it was the wrong thing to say. "If that's true, then why did she leave me all alone, letting me be passed from strange house to strange house while I wondered where she was?"

I don't have a good answer for that. I don't know what to say to comfort him. I lost my mother at thirteen, but it's not the same, and we both know it. I have memories of a woman who loved me and cared for me. Rafael has nothing but vague recollections.

"Doesn't matter," he says softly. "All that matters now is that we found our way to each other."

His words give me a little bit of hope that maybe we'll find a way to make this work. Even if it's a long-distance relationship, and we don't get to see each other much, that would be OK.

As long as he marries me, all will be well. We can do that, can't we? We can love each other across the oceans. Even as I think the thought, my heart fills with sorrow. I want to be with Rafael every day for the rest of my life.

If he asks me to choose between my duty and my heart, I'm not sure which one will win.

8

AURORA

THE NEXT MORNING, I WAKE UP ON FIRE. WHEN I open my eyes, I realize I'm not actually burning up. It's the warmth coming from Rafe's big body.

Last night after we made love two more times, he climbed into my sleeping bag with me. I don't know how the both of us managed to make it work, but we did. He's a restless sleeper who kept snoring. I may have *accidentally* elbowed him in the ribs once or twice to stop him from doing that. But each time I woke him, he gave me a soft smile and hugged me close.

I lean over and brush a strand of hair from his forehead. He stirs and murmurs sleepily, "Good morning."

Neither of us can hide the dopey grins on our faces. I've never felt like this before. I'm pretty sure I've fallen in love with the grumpy mountain man, and I think it's possible that he even loves me back.

My stomach growls, and he says, "I'll get breakfast going while you wash up."

I wash up and make a quick check-in call with Violet. I'm sure she hears the giddiness in my voice, but she doesn't comment on it. In fact, she barely asks me any questions. She's more distracted than usual and ends the conversation quickly.

After our call, I eat a quiet breakfast over the fire with Rafael. The entire time we're sitting side by side, and he's touching me in some small way. Whether it's putting his hand on my back or pressing his thigh against mine, he can't keep his hands off of me. I wonder if there was ever a point in my parents' marriage where they were like this. But I can't imagine Rafe is anything like my father.

"The lake here is so clear, so still," I tell him after we've finished our breakfast. "It reminds me of the one behind Father's castle."

"Do you go swimming in it often?"

I shake my head. "Oh no, it's not proper for a princess."

"There's no one here with us now." He makes a big show of looking around then he stands. He reaches for his shirt and tugs it over his head, revealing his beautiful body again.

He gives me a grin as he reaches for his pants, unbuttoning them. "Skinny dipping is a rite of passage. Everyone needs to do it at least once."

My cheeks grow warm. It doesn't matter that he's kissed every centimeter of my body and seen me naked in three different positions. I still can't believe I'm considering this, but I like the challenge in his gaze.

Before I can talk myself out of it, I push to my feet and shed my clothes too. We walk to the lake's banks, unashamed of our nakedness.

"On three." He threads his fingers through mine, his rough hand making me feel safe.

He counts softly under his breath then we're jumping into the clear blue lake together. The cold water is a shock to my system, and I break the surface with a grimace.

Rafe's head bobs up a second after mine.

"You didn't warn me it would be this cold." My teeth are chattering, and my nipples are hard points in the water.

He laughs, a booming, musical sound. "If I told you, it would have taken you twice as long to get in."

I flick water at him, and he flicks it back at me. Before I know it, we're chasing each other around the lake, diving under the water's cool surface and popping back up.

After a long morning of playing in the lake, I let him catch me. I grin, the arousal in his gaze makes me want him more. "You've caught me. Seems only right that you should get to plunder your treasure."

He grips my ass, bouncing me up and down. His cock rubs against my clit. "You like making me chase you, naughty girl."

I moan his name. "Please."

He slips inside of me and fills me with his shaft. He's so big and thick, and the way he grunts my name has my pussy clenching around him.

"I will always chase you," he growls. "Always hunt you down and ram into your tight little pussy."

I come at his filthy promises, feeling his release spurt into me. Slumping into his arms, I let him carry me onto the bank.

The afternoon sun is warm on my back as he sets me in the soft grass and pulls me close. We stay wrapped up in each other for long moments. It's late when I reach for my clothes and braid my hair.

He watches me as I do. He's wearing pants again, but they're not even buttoned. Seems a shame to keep his beautiful cock covered. One day, I want to lick it and explore his taste.

I put a hand on his knee. "Tell me."

I want to know everything in this man's head. I want to know all of his deepest thoughts and greatest fears. He's my favorite book, the one I want to reread again and again until I know every line by heart.

"You've told me what you don't like about your life, about the lack of freedom and the inability to do the things you want. But what do you like about it? Is there anything you love?"

I don't have to think long or hard to answer his question. "I love that I get to help so many of our kingdom's citizens. I love that I get to do so much social work. I love getting to paint in the tower, especially on those afternoons when the sun hits just right and everything in the room is bathed in a golden glow. Oh, and ball-room dancing! That's probably one of my favorite things."

"Ballroom dancing," he repeats, a dark expression comes over his face. "With other men."

I like that possessive glint in his eye, the way he

looks like he would kill another man for glancing in my direction.

I didn't realize how possessive he is or how much that would turn me on. The expression on his face is making my panties damp.

"I could teach you how to ballroom dance." I've never danced with anyone that makes me feel the way Rafe does. Something tells me that dancing with him will be different. Intimate. Special.

"You want to ballroom dance with me." I can't tell if the idea pleases him or upsets him. But it's too late to take the suggestion back now, so I shrug. "If you don't want to…"

He grabs my hip and squeezes it. "Teach me."

"We don't have any music."

He pulls his phone out and passes it to me with the music app open.

I select a soft song that's easy to learn to waltz to and tell him to close his eyes. "Hum along with me."

He does what I say and pretty soon our humming is synced to the song. "Do you hear that rhythm? The slow one…two…three of it."

When I open my eyes, I find him staring down at me with a look of awe and wonder on his face, like maybe he's seeing the whole universe in a glance. I hope that's true. I hope Rafael is as madly in love with me as I am with him.

"I got it, sweetheart." His voice is honey and sin, a deliciously tantalizing sound that has me wanting to pull him back onto the sleeping bags for another round of naked fun even as my heart warms at the pet name. "Now show me."

I position his body, pleased when he automatically grips me so tightly that his fingerprints are likely to be on my skin tomorrow. I want to always have his marks on me from the hickey that he sucked on the side of my neck to the beard burn between my thighs. I want the whole world to know that I belong to him. That he's marked me as his own.

He pulls me flush against his body, and I feel his arousal between us. He groans softly. "Fuck, being near your soft curves is heaven."

He stumbles through the song once and as we get to the end he says, "Again."

But by the third time we've gone through it, the steps are coming easier. Even though he's not a fluid dancer, he seems to be finding the rhythm of it.

"With more practice we'll make a proper dancer out of you yet," I tell him and lean up to give him a long kiss. I can't help it. There's something about this man. I always want to be touching him and kissing him just as much as he wants to always be touching and kissing me.

When I pull away, he doesn't look happy at all. Pain in his gaze. "Do you think we could be together, even though I'm not your prince?"

"You'll always be mine, prince or not." As soon as I say the words, I realize how true they are. If the monarchy rejects him, they'll be rejecting me too. We're one and what happens to him now happens to me.

His gaze drops back to my lips. I'm pretty sure he's going to ravage me again right here. But there are still a million things I want to learn about my man. "Can you tell me about the nightmares?"

I'm guessing that he has them, given how restless he was in the sleeping bag last night. He spoke at one point in his sleep, about a man coming for him in the dark but I couldn't make out the rest of what he was saying. It was too garbled.

He sighs and looks away, staring out at the lake. "I had them since I was a kid. Always this orange glow with a feeling of doom, like I couldn't breathe."

I reach out and touch his arm. I don't want him feeling alone in this. "Do you think it's anxiety?"

"I used to think that then the dreams started

changing. Right about the time you got here. Now there's a man in them. He's dark and I can't see his face. Hell, maybe it's my father. Whoever it is, he breathes funny. It's a weird noise."

I need to do some research later. Maybe Violet knows if Rafe's father ever had a breathing disorder. Maybe she can give us more insight into his family and why his kingdom doesn't seem to know anything about him.

Before I can suggest this, Rafe changes the subject. "What do you like to paint?"

I still have a million more questions for him about his past and the nightmares. But he's clearly done talking about it for now. "Still life mainly. You know, everyday items artfully arranged. I've been thinking about doing landscapes though. The mountains here are—"

His phone rings out, startling us from the moment. He steps away from me to pick up the phone and frowns at it.

"Is it Roman again?"

He nods. I suspect he's afraid of learning he is the prince.

"Go ahead," I encourage quietly. I already know in my heart what Roman is going to say. There's no way that Violet made a mistake. Rafael is a prince even if it's hard for him to acknowledge this.

He answers the call and listens for a moment before he says, "We'll be there in twenty minutes."

When he ends the conversation, his jaw is tight. He glances at me, a storm brewing in his Atlantic gaze. "It's time to learn if I really am your prince."

9

RAFE

THE BIRDS ARE CHIRPING. THE SKY IS BLUE WITH white fluffy clouds overhead, and woodland creatures are rustling in the forest. All around me the world is at peace, continuing to spin. But as I walk toward Roman's house, I feel like a man going to the gallows.

Beside me, Aurora slips her hand into mine. She gives it a gentle squeeze and looks up at me with such trust and devotion in her eyes. Could she be happy living as a simple mountain man's wife?

That's what I was really asking her back there when I wanted to know what she loved about her life. I'm no fool. I can't offer her the splendor she's used to. All I can give her is a warm bed and a man that will make her the center of his world.

"Whatever happens, it will be OK," she says this like what we're about to discover won't change everything between us. But of all people, I know that nothing in life is permanent. No one wants you forever, no matter how good you are or how much you try to please them.

I give her hand a gentle squeeze. I try to memorize how soft her fingers are against mine. Try to remember how beautiful she looks when the sun hits those freckles on her face and the way her dark eyes light up when she's in the throes of her pleasure.

By the time we arrive at Roman's cabin, some part of me is already preparing to let her go. Maybe it'll be easy. Maybe the moment she hears I'm not the prince, she'll reject me. There will be no long discussion, no tearful goodbyes. She'll simply walk out of my life, and I can pretend that she isn't walking out with my heart.

Roman opens the door at my knock and beckons us inside. The grim set of his mouth tells me I won't like what he found.

He points to the couch indicating that we should sit, but I can't sit. I need to be on my feet. I need to be moving. I pace the length of his living room, my boots clomping across the hardwood floors that he personally built.

Roman's construction business has done very well. He could live anywhere, but he's chosen a remote location in the mountains, and he only drives to work when necessary.

"What is it?" I bark.

He looks at me, and I'm almost certain that I see sympathy in his eyes. He's the big brother of our group, the oldest one and the man that looks out for everyone. Now he's turned his pity on me. It's almost more than I can stomach. "She's right. You're a prince."

I'm suddenly woozy. The ground underneath my feet is no longer solid. My voice grows louder and more insistent with each word. "If I were really a prince, I'd know it. And if I am the prince of the Republic of Wherever, then why has no one ever told me?"

"It's the Republic of Portia," he quietly corrects. "And your father believed in the eugenics movement. Are you familiar with it?"

From her place on the couch, Aurora gasps.

"It's that Nazi bullshit. What does it have to do with me?" I wave a hand, trying to understand his point.

"Well, the belief that a superior race can be bred was your father's whole world, so he thought—"

Before he can finish, the overwhelming realization hits me, and I feel nauseated. "Are you saying because I—" I gesture to my body, indicating my cerebral palsy.

Roman nods, jaw set firmly. "He wanted you gone, and your mother was unwilling to abandon you. Instead, she ran off with you in secret to the States. He started a smear campaign against her, and the whole kingdom bought into it. They thought your mother was a wicked woman who ran away with his heir and broke his heart."

"Surely, someone called him out on this...this insanity!" Aurora says, getting to her feet. Her hands are fisted against her thick hips.

"That's the thing about it," Roman continues, but he's not looking at her. It's me that he's watching. "You were kept from the public eye. From the first moment it was known that there was a problem, you were hidden away. There was speculation, but the king was careful. He only allowed a handful of trusted photographers to see you, always demanding that they capture the right angle. Nothing of your health was really known."

I think of those images I have of a dark-haired woman who tenderly cared for me and read bedtime stories. My knees nearly buckle. "Where is my mother? Can I meet her?"

This woman gave me life, and she brought me to another country with the hopes that I would be accepted.

"She passed away not long after your fourth birthday." He stops there, and I can tell there's more. Things he's not saying.

I fall to my knees. "It was a fire, wasn't it?"

The nightmares suddenly make sense. The orange glow that filled me with a sense of doom. It wasn't a dream. It happened.

"She didn't survive," I gasp out through a throat that's too tight. There was darkness so thick it was hard to breathe. The man coming toward me wasn't my father. He was a firefighter, his breathing apparatus was the funny noise I couldn't place. The man must have gotten me to safety.

There's pressure on my shoulder. Aurora is beside me, her hand squeezing my skin. She's grounding me, calling out my name the way you might a wounded animal.

Anger and despair war for control. We never would have been there if it weren't for him. If my father had accepted me, my mother would still be alive. I need someone to yell at, someone to curse. "Where is my father now?"

"He died a few years ago. But your brother, Mateo, is alive. He's on the throne. He's nothing like your father. He's a good man. One who fights for children's rights and champions those with disabilities." From the tone of Roman's voice, it's obvious he admires him, and that's a hard feat to pull off. Few men have ever gained Roman's admiration.

"How good can he be if he's never sought me out?" Betrayal lashes at me. Doesn't he miss me? Didn't he ever wonder where I went? Why my mother left him?

"They all rejected me. My own people. My family." Only my mom wanted me, and she's gone now.

Roman continues, "Upon your mother's death, your father made it look as if you too had died. There's a whole kingdom out there that doesn't even know you exist."

Aurora tries to put her arm around me, but I shrug away her touch. Pain flickers across her features, but I can't take in anything else. Every breath is a struggle, and this cabin is too small. "I have to get out of here."

I push to my feet and stomp out the door, leaving

her behind. I don't know how she'll get home. But I know Roman will look after her.

She storms after me and yells my name.

I stop and turn to her. Tears are streaming down her face, and it's a knife to the chest. There's too much pain competing for my attention.

"Rafael, wait. I want—"

"My name is Rafe," I grind out.

She reaches out a hand to touch me. I step away, not letting her make contact. I can't feel her hands on me right now. "Your father was a horrible person, but don't throw us away."

The anger consumes me, burning me from the inside out. "I don't want anything to do with any plan that came from him. Sorry about your kingdom, but you're on your own, princess."

With those words, I walk away, leaving her in the middle of the forest.

10

AURORA

I stare after his retreating figure. My heart is breaking in two. I thought I found forever with him. I thought he was meant to be. But now here I stand, rejected again.

Pain lances through my heart, deeper than anything I felt for my mother. Still, I recognize this pain so familiar. It's grief. Grief for what could have been, for what we lost.

My phone rings in my pocket, but he doesn't turn around. He's disappeared into the trees, and I fumble with my phone through my tears. Agony is making my fingers and heart numb.

When I see it's Violet, I answer immediately asking her, "What's wrong? Is it Father's health?"

Her voice is shaky, as if she's been crying. "You

must come home immediately, Princess. Your father's illness is getting worse."

"But Rafe—"

"It's too late. You have to come now," she insists.

I square my shoulders. I can't help Rafe through his pain. He's not willing to let me, but there is a kingdom that needs me. "I'll be there."

I end the call and turn in a circle, realizing that I don't know the way back.

Roman is standing on his porch, regarding me with a mixture of pity and compassion. "Give him time. He'll come around."

"There isn't time. I have to get home. Father is—" I press a hand to my mouth. It feels like everything is crashing down on me at once.

"Got it." He pulls his keys from his pocket. "Are you sure you don't want to try to say goodbye?"

The weight of the world rests on my too-tiny, too-frail shoulders. "He won't hear anything I say right now. He may never be ready to hear me."

I can't imagine how deep is pain must be. All those times he thought he wasn't good enough. Now it seems as if his worst fears have been confirmed.

I wish he would let me in, that he would allow me to go through this with him. But he's rejected me. He's rejected my love, and I can't wait. Nico will use this opportunity to take the crown.

I look to Roman and give him a resolute nod. All I can do at this point is stay focused on saving my kingdom. I can't think about how the love of my life walked away from me.

Roman drives me to the airport in stony silence. I appreciate the fact that he doesn't try to drag me into conversation.

As we near the airport, his vehicle makes a clunking noise, and I look to him. Guilt flickers across his features. "I guess, it backfired on me this time."

"What do you mean?"

He doesn't answer me. He mutters something about it would teach him to sabotage his own vehicle. Still, we manage to arrive at the airport safely, and it's then I realize I have no money or means. I lost my return ticket in the rain with my luggage. As it is, I'm lucky to have my phone and passport.

"Don't worry. I gotcha," Roman reassures me when he realizes I don't have the funds.

"I'll repay you," I promise. I saw how he regarded Rafe with such brotherly affection, the way it hurt him to disclose his past.

"Repay me by waiting for him. He loves you.

Give him time to get his head on straight." He gives me a brief hug. It's over so quickly that I almost think I imagined it. Then he's gone, melting into the crowd.

I take the ticket and board the commercial flight, knowing that my life as a commoner is officially over. I'll never get to live like this again. Never get to feel Rafe's arms around me.

As I leave American soil, I'm leaving half my heart behind. It amazes me that when I landed on this continent, all I could think about was the heavy feeling in the pit of my stomach. The knowledge that I was shackling myself to one man for the rest of my life. One man who might be cold and cruel. But I arrived and found him kind. He was compassionate. He was quiet and funny, and he made me feel like I mattered.

My heart has stopped beating. My blood no longer circulates. I can't even draw in oxygen. There's only the cold nothingness of having lost love.

When the plane touches down on Velkan soil, I am home and yet for the first time in my life, Velkan is not home. My home is Rafe.

Violet greets me with an uncharacteristically warm show of emotion, folding me into a hug. As I gaze into her eyes, it strikes me that she looks as if she's aged thirty years. "Your father has passed on."

It's the first time she's called him that instead of the king. I don't know what to say to the news. I don't know how to process this. He didn't feel like my father. He was more of a stranger that I'd desperately hoped would one day grow to love me.

"I couldn't convince Rafe to come with me." My throat is raw like I've swallowed razor blades. "But if we can find another suitable groom..." The words are vile on my tongue. I will never love another man. Rafe was—he still is—my soulmate. Even if we are never together.

She nods. The look she gives me is somehow stern and reassuring at the same time. "We can't let the kingdom fall to Nico. I will select another groom for you."

Ice flows through my veins. I've fallen into a river of heartbreak. It's cold and consuming. I'm certain that I'm going to drown in the depths. "The sooner I can announce my nuptials, the better."

Rafe

THE SUN HAS SET BY THE TIME I REALIZE WHAT I'VE done. I've spent all day staring into this lake, pondering my life and all the choices that led me here.

No matter what my father was or what he did, he managed to do one thing right. He created the betrothal agreement between me and Aurora.

My chest aches as soon as I think of her, and I rub a hand against my sternum to ease the pain. Did I really do that? Did I really send her away?

The image of her hurt expression washes over me. I was angry. I wasn't thinking clearly. In my anger, I wounded her. The only woman I can imagine spending forever with, and I let her slip through my fingers.

I race back to Roman's cabin. It's dark, but he's on the porch. He's sipping a mug of coffee with Hale, another of the neighboring mountain men. They're having a quiet conversation. Sounds like they're discussing his truck that needs to go into the shop. Either Roman bought the worst clunker in the country, or he has a thing for Gabby, the pretty mechanic who works at the auto shop.

"Where is she?" I demand, looking for Aurora.

Roman sets his mug down. "I drove her to the airport hours ago."

"She's gone?" For the second time today, everything tilts. I struggle to find solid ground. She's my whole world. She can't be gone.

Hale stands from his rocking chair, pausing to roll the kinks out of his neck. "She got a call. Her father is dying."

"I have to go to her." I can't stand the idea that she's facing this alone. She has to know I'll be there for her. She doesn't face life alone anymore. I'll be by her side now. Always.

"The plane has already touched down. She's back in her country. Are you sure that's not for the best?" Roman is studying me intently. "Are you ready to be part of her world? You're not talking about going overseas. You're talking about giving up your citizenship here. You'll be starting a brand-new life, adapting to a different culture."

His words don't even make me flinch. "I can't imagine life without her by my side. I'll do whatever it takes, but I have to go now. She needs me. If I miss my chance…" I can't finish the thought. It's too horrible to contemplate. I'm certain that my heart will stop beating if I can't find Aurora. If I can't tell her I love her and hold her in my arms every day for the rest of my life.

"We don't have long," Roman says and he stands too.

Hale grabs the bags on the porch. "Brennon loaned us his plane. Flight plan has already been filed. All we've been waiting for is you to get your head on straight."

Within an hour, the three of us are in the air. Even Herbert has come along for the ride. I couldn't leave him behind. The cabin can be replaced, and I can get new things. But he's been my buddy for years.

Even though the plane ride only takes a few hours, it feels like three decades. I can't talk to Aurora or get in touch with her while we're midflight. The moment we're on the ground, I'm racing through the private airport. But I stop in front of the TV and gasp in horror. There's a ticker at the bottom announcing the king has passed away. Her dad died and I wasn't there for her. She's about to go through one of the hardest times of her life, and she needs me.

"I have to get to her. We need to find a way into the palace," I tell my friends.

"Calm down, Rambo," Hale says, looking at me with amusement. "We've already got you covered."

I look to Roman who nods as suited men approach us. "We have an escort in."

Our friend Brennon is a billionaire and Roman has considerable pull, but even they don't have enough to get me into the palace. He claps me on the shoulder. "There are advantages to being the long-lost prince."

"My brother knows about me." My only thought has been getting to my girl. I haven't even thought about the possibility of meeting my older brother.

Roman shrugs. "As soon as I got the report, I sent your DNA to be compared. I wanted to make certain before I told you. As soon as the confirmation came in, Mateo insisted on sending men to guard you."

Roman had my back, and I'll always be grateful for that. "Gotta warn you though. Violet is not too happy about your arrival. Woman is as warm as a rattlesnake, but she'll let you into the castle."

The security team has reached us, and the men bow to me. They even address me as your highness which causes me to scowl at them. I don't like being treated differently, never have. But if this is the price of entry into her world, I'll accept it.

Within minutes, we're whisked to the palace, and I find myself standing before Violet. She squares her shoulders when she sees me. "Before you go any further—"

"I'm coming to see her. I'll tear this palace down brick by brick if that's what it takes."

To my surprise, she doesn't try to argue with me. She presses her lips together and points behind her. "Through that door."

That's when I start running because I can't imagine not being near my curvy woman for one more minute.

11
AURORA

He's come to gloat. Nico says he's here to pay his respects, but we both know what the gleam in his eye really means. He thinks he's won, that he'll be crowned the next king within the week.

I pretend to accept his condolences because I can't risk tipping my hand. I even have him for tea. The entire time, he keeps glancing around the room. He's already planning how to redecorate the palace to appeal to his whores.

I haven't slept in the past twenty-four hours. I've barely eaten, and my heart is raw in my chest. But I've gone on national television and declared a week of mourning for my late father and authorized the burial preparations.

I've already done this once before with my mom,

but it was different. I was so close to her. It was like losing my best friend. With Father, there's only grief for the warm relationship we could have had.

"How is Jasmine?" I despise Nico, but his wife is kind. She's the one good thing about the man, but lately, she's been having horrible migraines. It's why she's not with him today.

"Attention seeking as usual." He flicks a piece of lint off his dress pants. "How is Rafe? Sorry, Rafael. Did you have a good visit?"

I take a sip of my tea, refusing to show him any emotion. I don't understand how he knows anything about Rafe but given how often he's visited Father in the past months, he's probably made friends within the castle walls.

"It couldn't have been that cordial, seeing how you're here. *Single*." He pretends to drum his fingers on his knees. "Only a few days left before Velkan's new reigning monarch will be announced."

I want to smack the smirk off his face. Instead, I keep my tone neutral. "I look forward to the announcement."

"I look forward to seeing you on your knees for me."

I set my teacup down. It clinks loudly against my saucer. "Listen, you little conniving—"

Before I can finish my statement, there's the sound of yelling. Someone is yelling my name and racing down the hall. There are other heavy footsteps, as if they're being chased.

I push to my feet. There's the sudden sound of many men running toward me. My heart pounds as I imagine that this might be the coup that Nico has been planning. But why would he do this when he's so close to getting everything he's wanted?

Instead of armed man bursting into the door, it's one man. It's Rafe, and I recognize the fire in his eyes. It's the same look he had on the banks of the lake. "What are you doing here?"

"I warned you I would chase you down." He storms across the tearoom, pushes me against the wall, and kisses me passionately. His lips against mine are perfect. Despite the fact that I should be angry with him for rejecting me, I can't help but melt against him. It's been twenty-four hours without his kisses, without his scowls, without his teasing and his dry sense of humor.

"I fucked up." Those are the first words out of his mouth when he lifts his head long enough for both of us to desperately drag in some oxygen.

"It's okay. I've missed you." My fingers are curled into his shirt. I'm afraid if I let him go, he'll disappear like a puff of smoke. This can't be real, can it?

He thrusts something between us and that's when I realize the yellow blur from earlier was flowers. Sunflowers. My heart melts.

"If you give me another chance, I promise to plant you fields of sunflowers. I promise to walk with you through every day, the good and the bad. But more than that, I promise to love you every day for the rest of our lives. Aurora, you're the queen of my heart. Would you make me the happiest man on earth by marrying me?" His eyes are shining with such sincerity and love. I know that whatever happens between us, this man will love me forever.

Tears are streaming from my eyes as I throw my arms around his shoulders. I press kisses to his neck as I tell him how much I love him and how happy he makes me.

"I will challenge the monarchy if you marry this...this...*commoner!*" Nico spits out the word, like it's something foul and dirty.

But Rafe is unfazed. He cups my face and looks at me with such tenderness in his gaze. "I don't know if they'll honor our commitment. But I promise I will."

"You can't marry her! She's—"

Before Nico can finish the insult, Rafe turns and

lands a solid punch to his jaw. He glares at my smarmy cousin. "This woman is not just your future queen, she's my future wife. And no one talks disrespectfully about her or to her."

Nico falls to the floor clutching his chin and whimpering. One of his bodyguards tries to approach Rafe, but all my mountain man has to do is send him a menacing look. The other man quickly backs down.

"Everyone out!" Rafe roars. The men that came with him glance around before they leave. Nico and his bodyguard scurry from the room with my cousin muttering threats under his breath the entire time.

He takes the flowers from me, carefully setting them on a nearby table before he stalks back toward me, something feral in his expression.

"I told you what would happen if you ran from me, princess," Rafe growls as he flips up my skirt and exposes my panties. Moisture gushes between my legs. That same look that was there at the lake is back. His eyes glitter with something dark. He needs to possess me, to make me his in every way.

He runs his nose along the column of my throat, inhaling my scent. "Do you remember what I said?"

I shiver as he slips a hand under my shirt and

into my bra. He palms my breast with one hand. "I can't recall it."

It's a lie, and we both know it. Those words are tattooed on my brain.

"Liar." He tweaks my nipple. Hard. "Say it. Tell me what happens to you now."

I gasp, loving this side of him. I had no idea that Rafe could be so demanding. "You said you would hunt me down and ram into my tight little pussy."

"That's right." He yanks down my panties with his other hand, exposing my needy pussy to the cool air. I'm so slick between my thighs that it should be embarrassing. But the way Rafe came in here and took control of the room and more importantly, my body has only made him hotter.

He crams his fingers into my tight hole and curses. "You need this, don't you, sweetheart?"

All I can do is whimper my agreement as my hips buck. My body is trying desperately to ride his hand. My body knows exactly who gives me pleasure.

"So much cream." He pulls away his glistening fingers and shoves them at my lips. "Taste it."

I wrap my lips around his blunt digit and suck, hollowing my cheeks. I swirl my tongue around his finger and imagine it's his cock instead. I imagine he's pushing the broad head inside of me, that he's whispering filthy things to me as he touches the back of my throat.

He swears and pulls his finger away, making a wet popping noise. He yanks his cock from his pants and pumps it twice. "I'll put you on your knees next time. You'll be a good little cocksucker, won't you?"

I whimper my agreement and writhe against his body, my release so close. "Please, Rafe…"

He doesn't go slow and sweet like he was in the tent. No, my mountain man rams into my tight channel in one forceful stroke. My body tightens at the invasion but he slips a hand between us, petting my clit. "Take it deep. There you go. Such a good girl for me."

His words have me preening even as he hammers into me. I love the way he's playing me so skillfully, demanding my pleasure.

"Put your legs around my hips." He grunts. "Gonna work your little pussy until you remember who owns it."

"You do!" I cry out as I work my legs up the way he wants. Not only is he so deep that I feel every pulse of his thick cock, but now I'm trapped between his big body and the wall. I can only take what he gives me, only accept the pleasure that he's forcing onto me.

When he reaches for my clit again, I detonate on the spot. The orgasm is so intense that only when it's over and my throat is sore do I realize I was screaming. Everyone in this part of the castle just heard me scream his name. Even Violet. The thought makes my cheeks heat.

"Everyone knows," I whisper to him.

"Damn straight they do," Rafe answers as he spills into me. "Now everyone knows who makes the queen come, whose cock she bounces on."

I flush even deeper and despite the fact that he's stopped thrusting, neither of us try to move. It feels so good with his cock lodged deep inside of me. His come is leaking from my body, proof that he's marked me.

"Now," he rasps out the word. "I want to get married now."

I chuckle. He's still buried balls-deep in me. I have no doubts about marrying Rafe. I know that he's everything I want in a man. I'll be proud to be the queen next to this king. "Are you sure?"

He may have been saying filthy things to me only seconds ago but the warmth in his gaze right now melts me. "There's no reason to wait. You're the other half of my heart. I don't know how it was decided that we would be together. But I'm damn glad for that betrothal. You've been mine since the day you were born, and that's how it is, sweetheart."

I grin up at him, happiness making me giddy. "Then yes, I will marry you right now. But maybe I could get some clean panties first."

AURORA

"I KNOW THAT TRADITION DICTATES MY FATHER should walk me down the aisle. But even if he were here, I'd rather it be you." I glance in the mirror at Violet.

She's the one who spent nearly every waking moment of her life supporting me. She's helped me learn how to navigate the life of a royal, comforted me as I grieved my mother, and loved me through it all.

The soft smile on her face tells me how flattered she is by my request. "Of course, Princess."

There will be an official wedding in a few months. But for now, Rafe and I will marry here in the castle. Our quiet ceremony will be everything I imagined it to be. It will give us the chance to start our life together as man and wife.

Sure, there are some who will question me marrying so soon after my father's passing. It's not that my marriage magically fixes it. There will always be a bit of grief when I think of him and the father that I wish he had been.

Violet adjusts the sparkly tiara on my head one more time then we walk down the short corridor to the dining room. It's been temporarily transformed into our wedding chapel.

It was strange facing everyone after I'd just been freshly fucked. Everyone knew it, but no one said a word. I'm sure that was in part Violet's doing. She's always managed to keep everything within the castle walls running smoothly.

Besides, the staff was delighted to assist in my sudden nuptials, and I can't deny how happy it made me to have so many people support me during this time. I can only hope that in the coming days and weeks, I'll be a queen worthy of more than their love and admiration. I want to earn the respect of my people and show them how deeply I care for our country.

"Your mother would be so proud of you." Violet passes me my bouquet of sunflowers that are wrapped with a cheerful red ribbon. She really did think of everything.

She takes my arm in hers. She's been my steady rock, and I have to swallow the lump in my throat. She's been a grandmother, mentor, and friend all wrapped into one.

"Thank you," I manage to murmur and blink to keep from ruining my makeup. Not that it helps much because when I look up, Rafe is staring back at me. The intensity and love shining in his gaze take my breath away. After years of craving affection, I never thought I would find it with this gruff mountain man.

I still can't believe I'm marrying him, this guy who wants to plant a field of sunflowers for me, who takes me camping because it makes me happy, and chases me down in the cool lake water so he can claim me.

It's a good thing that Violet is beside me as I move toward him because I'm pretty sure if she weren't here, I'd be running to this man and throwing myself into his arms.

The ceremony is simple and short. Rafe promises to love and protect me above all others and seals the words with a traditional gold band. Then he kisses me and scoops me into his arms, carrying me straight into the bridal suite at the end of the hall.

"You're so beautiful," Rafe tells me as he undresses me from my wedding gown. The look of adoration in his eyes has me feeling like the sexiest woman in the world. He's not the same feral beast he was earlier. Now he's softer, gentler, calmer. I think knowing I'm his has calmed him. At least, for now.

"You looked pretty handsome yourself today, husband," I give him a wink as I sink down onto the plush bed. The silk is cool against my overheated skin as I watch him pull off his suit.

"Never going to get tired of hearing you call me husband." He stretches out over me and lets out a hiss when our bodies connect. He gazes down at me, tenderness and love filling his expression. "You're my forever."

I cup his face. "And you're mine."

He slips inside my body, filling me with the most delicious stretch. I groan when he starts to move, a gentle rhythm that has me raising my hips to meet his. When we come, it's together in a sweaty heap that has him collapsing next to me in the bed.

Rafe puts my head on his chest and pulls me close. I love it when we're like this, the two of us alone together naked. But there's a world outside of this room, and it won't wait more than a day. Maybe two at the most if Violet can buy us that much time. I finally think of all the things we didn't discuss before this. "We'll be coronated soon."

"*You* will be coronated soon," he answers with a sleepy yawn. I wonder if he's missed as much sleep as I have. He's definitely looking like it with those dark circles under his eyes.

My heart sinks. "You're my husband."

"And a very happy one at that," he practically purrs the words, leaving me no doubt that he's been fully sated.

"That would make you the king," I point out. "We'll share the duties, the power, the leadership. Everything."

He's quiet for a long moment. "Didn't consider that."

"I know you don't want to be royalty, and—"

He tucks a strand of hair behind my ear. "Sitting on a throne does not appeal to me. But I'll do whatever it takes to be with you. At the end of the day, it's a title. What I care about is being there for my woman."

I blink back moisture at his words. He always knows what to say to make me feel loved.

"To the rest of the world we'll be the King and Queen," he says, "but in here it's you and me."

I smile against his chest and close my eyes, sleep overtaking me after the whirlwind of the past few days.

THE NEXT MORNING, THERE'S A KNOCK ON THE DOOR.

Violet enters the room after I give permission. It strikes me then that she always used to knock and enter without waiting. But things are different now because I'm a married woman. Rafe is in the bathroom, brushing his teeth.

Violet's gaze flicks over me, probably noting all the places with beard burn. There's not a centimeter of my skin that my mountain man didn't spend the night sucking and nibbling and licking. "I'm sorry. I waited as long as possible before I had to disturb you."

I wrap a robe around myself. "What is it?"

I know that Rafe and I didn't exactly pick the ideal time to get married. Between my father's passing and the sudden discovering of the Republic of Portia's new prince, there will be a lot of questions to answer and many details to attend.

Before she can answer, Rafe steps out of the bathroom. She drops her gaze when she realizes he isn't wearing a shirt. She bows, murmuring quietly, "Your Highness."

Rafe scowls at me, and I look to Violet. "Not behind closed doors."

She straightens. "I have come to notify you both that Your Highness—Rafael—your brother awaits you in the dining hall."

"What?" He gasps out.

"I apologize. We could not hold him much longer. King Mateo has been eager to meet you since the moment he heard of your existence. We could send him away but the ensuing political turmoil would be—"

Rafe sighs. "This is not political for me."

Violet has the decency to look apologetic. "Of course, I didn't mean to imply that it should be."

Rafe scratches his beard. He's probably as nervous about meeting his brother as he is about what he might discover.

I reach for his hand, threading his fingers through mine and focus my attention on Violet. "Keep him entertained for fifteen more minutes, then we'll be there."

Relief flickers across Rafe's face, and I know this

was the right move. But that's the thing about being married. We no longer fight our own battles. Now we stand shoulder to shoulder always supporting each other and lifting each other up.

He watches me get ready, his gaze hungry. "I should make him wait another twenty minutes so I can ravage my wife."

"Or meet your brother, and your wife will take care of you later." I waggle my eyebrows so there's no doubt about what I mean.

Together, we walk hand in hand to meet with Rafe's brother. The moment I enter the dining room, there's no doubt in my mind that they're brothers. They have similar features, except that Rafe is taller, and Mateo has far more gray hair around his temples. It makes me think about growing old with Rafael, and I smile at the thought

Neither of them speaks for a long moment. Finally, I approach his brother, King Mateo. "We're glad you're here."

"I came as soon as I heard the news." He shakes his head. "All this time. I thought you were dead."

Rafe's voice is gruff when he speaks, and I know how much emotion my stoic man is fighting back against. "I had no idea. I was raised with no knowledge of you or my country."

Then to my surprise, Rafe throws his arms around the other man and pulls him close.

"Brother," Mateo exclaims.

I see the word as it hits Rafe. The way his face lights up at the knowledge he has family. My mountain man is no longer alone. He has family around him now.

They spend hours swapping stories from their lives, and by the time Mateo is called away on urgent matters for Portia, they're exchanging phone numbers. They'll visit again as often as their schedules allow.

Rafe waits until his brother has gone to pull me into his arms and press a soft kiss to my forehead. "Thank you for being there."

I beam up at him. "There are a few ways you can thank me, husband."

He tosses me over his shoulder and I laugh as he speed walks down the corridor. Whatever the future holds, Rafe and I will face it together. After all, we're a team.

EPILOGUE

RAFE

"No peeking," I tell my wife as I guide her behind the castle. We've been walking for a few minutes, but the suspense is driving her wild.

I pause in front of a tree branch, using gentle pressure on her hand, and she instantly stills. I guide her over the branch.

She chuckles, a throaty sound that goes straight to my cock. We've been together for over a year now, and I still can't get enough of this woman. Everything she does is sexy to me. I spend my days running around the castle behind her, eager to catch my little whirlwind and remind her of just how much her king adores her. She's fierce and powerful, a force to be reckoned with.

Since becoming the queen, she has decreased

poverty rates throughout the capital city. She's also struck a lucrative commerce deal with the Republic of Portia. She still paints, mainly at my insistence. She tried to give up the hobby a few months ago, telling me she was too busy to do it anymore.

I won't let her lose herself to the crown. It's just a position, but she's my wife. I make sure she gets time away for painting and horseback riding. Moxie is a good friend to my woman, and she makes her smile on the days when her responsibilities are heavy.

At least once a month, I take Aurora to visit Mateo. Though my schedule and his are incredibly busy, we both make spending time together a priority.

I've had the chance to meet his wife and my little nephew. Seeing the three of them together made me eager to start a family with my bride. Even now, the thought of putting my baby in her makes my cock even harder behind my zipper. It's a permanent condition. I'm always hard, always aching to slide into her warm pussy.

"Where are we going?" She asks again for the hundredth time. Since watching her become queen, I've learned my woman thrives on being in control, and I don't mind. Except when it comes to the bedroom. Then I'm the one in control. Last night, I pinned her down to the bed and spent hours keeping her on edge until she was flushed and begging for my cock.

I don't answer for a moment, guiding her body around the enclosure for Herbert. I worried the new environment would be rough on him, but his body has adapted to the cooler temperatures here in Velkan. Since the move, he's as grumpy and aloof as always, which I take to be a good sign.

"Rafe, if you take me blindfolded and dump me into the lake, I will never forgive you," she says. She probably means it too. Except that I'm pretty sure I could calm her down eventually with orgasms.

Despite the protocols of the palace, she and I frequent the lake. Some evenings when the sun is dropping low in the sky and the stars are beginning to wink out in the darkness, I take her skinny dipping.

I love those moments with her when it's the two of us. Maybe one day we'll be lucky and it will be the three of us. The idea makes something in my chest ache. "I wouldn't do that to you, promise."

I have tossed my bride into the lake a few times, but I've never done it when she was blindfolded.

I pause in the clearing a few feet from the lake. I know she can hear the water and the soft sound of the crickets singing their nightly love songs. It's a perfect night, a clear one with hundreds of stars overhead. Something about being under the sky at night helps us to remember how insignificant most of our problems are. We use the stars to find our balance again, remembering that we are not eternal like they are.

While she's been busy with commerce and poverty relief programs, I've found my own way to make myself useful to the kingdom. I've been working with the agricultural department to launch an initiative that will help farmers grow a wider range of crops. Turns out, the terrain in Velkan is a lot like the mountains of Courage County which means I have insights to offer.

The people have accepted me as more than just their king. They see me as one of their own, a farmer just like them. After so long wandering the world alone, it feels good to find the place where I'm wanted and treated as family. In fact, the whole country reminds me of Courage.

A few months after we were married, Aurora and I snuck away to spend time there together. I know she's itching to go back so I haven't sold the cabin. I pay a housekeeper to maintain the place, and we treat it as our vacation home.

Aurora makes a little noise of impatience. She's always so eager to be in motion, to be doing something. If I didn't calm her down every night before bed with orgasms, I swear this woman would never sleep. Not that I mind. It's a hell of a sleep aid for both of us.

I reach for the blindfold and tug it gently from her face, though I make a note to use it on her again later. I saw the way it made her eyes dilate and her nipples pebble when I first put it on her. My woman likes the idea of being blindfolded and at my mercy.

She blinks her eyes open and glances around. I know the moment she spots the yellow tent that I've set up along with the firepit. Her expression softens, and she looks up at me.

I see the tears she tries to blink back. She's been teary a lot more than usual lately, and I make a note to mention that to Violet.

Violet keeps swearing that she's going to retire, but I don't think she ever will. Despite the way she fusses over me and my wife, she loves being around us.

"You did this for me," Aurora says. She swallows hard. Over the past year, she's mentioned how much she loved that night together in the tent. She called it one of the happiest moments of her life, and tonight on the anniversary of our wedding, I wanted to remind her of all the good times we've had together. I know there will be plenty more to look forward to in the future. But sometimes it's good to look back and remember all the things we shared together.

We settle by the fire and when I produce chocolate bars for s'mores she burst out into tears. I drop the unopened candy onto the ground and scoot closer to her on the log.

I wrap my arms around her and pull her into my lap. She's been under a lot of stress lately. My woman is strong, and she can handle anything this world throws at her, but she doesn't handle it alone. I rub a hand down her back and let her cry it out.

Before I can ask her what's wrong, she says, "I'm so happy."

"I'll always make sure your tears are happy ones." It's a promise I've made many times, and it's one I intend to keep every day for the rest of our lives.

"This was a really cool anniversary gift, and you won't even get to see my gift for months." She takes my hand and puts it to her stomach.

Emotion clogs my throat, making it hard to speak. I lift my eyebrows, questioning if this is what I think it is. Is she really giving me a baby? Is she making me a daddy?

She nods and I press a gentle kiss to her forehead. "This is the best gift you could have given me."

"I'm glad you like it," she says softly. "I was nervous. We've never talked about this and—"

"I want all the babies you're willing to give me. I don't care whether we have one kid or a dozen. I want you to be happy."

"I am happy," she answers. "So happy."

I tuck her into my arms, resting my chin on her head and inhaling her special scent. I don't know how I got so lucky. But I know that I'll always be thankful for the princess that stumbled into my cabin that night and the life we're building together.

Want a bonus scene with Rafe and Aurora? Sign up for my weekly newsletter and get the bonus here.

READ NEXT: BRED BY THE MOUNTAIN MAN

This filthy mountain man is determined to breed the curvy woman who fuels his darkest fantasies...

Gabby

It's not breaking and entering when you use a key. Or feed his fish and water his house plants. I'm just being neighborly. That's what you do in a small town like Courage County.

Sure, there are some people who try to scare me off from Roman, the savage mountain man. I know the rumors that swirl around him.

He's done hard time. He's gruff and grumpy. He's also...lonely. I don't know how I know that. I just know that I do. Maybe that's why I keep showing up at his place and doing nice things for him.

Except one day he comes home early and catches me in the act. Now the older mountain man is insisting that he'll put a ring on my finger and his babies in my belly.

Roman

I've been obsessed with Gabby since the day I met her. The petite mechanic changes the oil and rotates the tires of my truck. But what I really want is to get under her hood because there's only one thing those curves were built for: making babies.

But the curvy woman deserves better than a big brute like me. So I keep my distance until the day I can't. The day I come home to find her cleaning up my place and making me a hot meal. It's time to turn her into my dirty little housewife, so I can finally breed her sexy body.

If you love a dominant, filthy mountain man who's determined to love (and breed) his curvy woman, it's time to meet Roman in Bred by the Mountain Man.

Read Roman and Gabby's Story

COURAGE COUNTY SERIES

Welcome to Courage County where protective alpha heroes fall for strong curvy women they love and defend. There's NO cheating and NO cliffhangers. Just a sweet, sexy HEA in each book.

Love on the Ranch

Her Alpha Cowboy

Pregnant and alone, Riley has nowhere to go until the alpha cowboy finds her. Will she fall in love with her rescuer?

Her Older Cowboy

Summer is making a baby with her brother's best friend. But he insists on making it the old-fashioned way.

Her Protector Cowboy

Jack will do whatever it takes to protect his curvy woman after their hot one-night stand...then he plans to claim her!

Her Forever Cowboy

Dean is in love with his best friend's widow. When they're stranded together for the night, will he finally tell her how he feels?

Her Dirty Cowboy

The ranch's newest hire also happens to be the woman Adam had a one-night stand with...and she's carrying his baby!

Her Sexy Cowboy

She's a scared runaway with a baby. He's determined to protect them both. But neither of them expected to fall in love.

Her Wild Cowboy

He'll keep his curvy woman safe, even if it means a marriage in name only. But what happens when he wants to make it a real marriage?

Her Wicked Cowboy

One hot night with Jake gave me the best gift of my life: a beautiful baby girl. Will he want us to be a family when I show up on his doorstep a year later?

Courage County Brides

The Cowboy's Bride

The only way out of my horrible life is to become a mail order bride. But will my new cowboy husband be willing to take a chance on love?

The Cowboy's Soulmate

Can a jaded playboy find forever with his curvy mail order bride and her baby? Or will her secret ruin their future?

The Cowboy's Valentine

I'm a grumpy loner cowboy and I like it that way. Until my beautiful mail order bride arrives and suddenly, I want more than a marriage in name only.

The Cowboy's Match

Will this mail order bride matchmaker take a chance on love when she falls for the bearded cowboy who happens to be her VIP client?

The Cowboy's Obsession

Can this stalker cowboy show the curvy schoolteacher that he's the one for her?

The Cowboy's Sweetheart

Rule #1 of becoming a mail order bride: never fall in love with your cowboy groom.

The Cowboy's Angel

Can this cowboy single dad with a baby find love with his new mail order bride?

The Cowboy's Heiress

This innocent heiress is posing as a mail order bride. But what happens when her grumpy cowboy husband discovers who she really is?

Courage County Warriors

Rescue Me

Getting out was hard. Knowing who to trust was easy: my dad's best friend. He's the only man I can count on, but will we be able to keep our hands off each other?

Protect Me

When I need a warrior to protect me, I know just who to turn to: my brother's best friend. But will this grumpy cowboy who's guarding my body break my heart?

Shield Me

When trouble comes for me, I know who to call—my ex-boyfriend's dad. He's the only one who can help. But can I convince this grumpy cowboy to finally claim me?

Courage County Fire & Rescue

The Firefighter's Curvy Nanny

As a single dad firefighter, I was only looking for a quick fling. Then the curvy woman from last night shows up. Turns out, she's my new nanny.

The Firefighter's Secret Baby

After a scorching one-night stand with a sexy firefighter, I realize I'm pregnant...with my brother's best friend's baby.

The Firefighter's Forbidden Fling

I knew a one night stand with my grumpy boss wasn't the best idea...but I didn't think it would lead to anything serious. I definitely didn't think it would lead to a surprise pregnancy with this sexy firefighter.

GET A FREE COWBOY ROMANCE

Get Her Grumpy Cowboy for FREE:
https://www.MiaBrody.com/free-cowboy/

LIKE THIS STORY?

If you enjoyed this story, please post a review about it. Share what you liked or didn't like. It may not seem like much, but reviews are so important for indie authors like me who don't have the backing of a big publishing house.

Of course, you can also share your thoughts with me via email if you'd prefer to reach out that way. My email address is mia @ miabrody.com (remove the spaces). I love hearing from my readers!

ABOUT THE AUTHOR

Mia Brody writes steamy stories about alpha men who fall in love with big, beautiful women. She loves happy endings and every couple she writes will get one!

When she's not writing, Mia is searching for the perfect slice of cheesecake and reading books by her favorite instalove authors.

Keep in touch when you sign up for her newsletter: https://www.MiaBrody.com/news. It's the fastest way to hear about her new releases so you never miss one!

50791466R00086